GREAT IRISH SPORTS STARS

AYEISHA McFERRAN

DAVID CAREN is the writer of the bestselling parenting book
The Irish Dad's Survival Guide to Pregnancy [and Beyond] ... A real
bona fide hockey dad to three teenage hockey players, when not
running his own 'running' business, David is often seen pitchside
at his kids' matches, or wrestling his eldest daughter's hockey goalie
kit into the boot space of his Mini Cooper.

GREAT IRISH SPORTS STARS

AYEISHA McFERRAN

DAVID CAREN

THE O'BRIEN PRESS
DUBLIN

First published 2022 by
The O'Brien Press Ltd,
12 Terenure Road East, Rathgar,
Dublin 6, D06 HD27 Ireland.
Tel: +353 1 4923333; Fax: +353 1 4922777
E-mail: books@obrien.ie.
Website: obrien.ie.
The O'Brien Press is a member of Publishing Ireland

ISBN: 978-1-78849-281-2

8 7 6 5 4 3 2 1
26 25 24 23 22

Printed in the UK by Clays Ltd, St Ives plc.
The paper in this book is produced using pulp from managed forests.

Published in:

CONTENTS

CHAPTER I

OLYMPIC DREAMS

Ayeisha could not sleep. The sound of the rain rattling on the window was keeping her awake.

Lying in her comfy king size bed in the Sandymount Hotel, she stared up at the ceiling. She had gone to bed early, wanting to be rested for Ireland's second match against Canada. The first match, earlier that evening, had finished scoreless.

Ayeisha was still in awe of the 6,000 Irish supporters who had braved the wet, cold November weather to cheer on the Green Army – it had been the biggest turnout ever for an Irish hockey match.

Energia Park in Donnybrook, once the home of Leinster Rugby, had been fully transformed to host the two-day hockey Olympic qualifier between Ireland and Canada. A blue 'pop-up' carpet had been cleverly placed over the rugby field, transforming it into a hockey pitch.

Ayeisha closed her eyes and prayed that tomorrow would bring a win for Ireland, and better weather! With a win against Canada, they would be off to Tokyo, to play against the best hockey teams in the world at the Olympic games.

She woke early with great excitement. After stretching and showering, she joined her Irish teammates for breakfast. There was a sea of green shirts in the hotel dining room.

'Today is the day, Ayeisha,' Róisín Upton whispered, appearing beside the Irish goalkeeper.

'I'll be ready once I have my porridge, Róis,' Ayeisha winked.

The coach trip to Energia Park was a short one, but that didn't stop the team from singing. 'Go Green Army, Go Green Army,' they roared as the team bus turned into the grounds.

The mood was altogether different in the dressing room. The team listened intently as Coach Sean Dancer delivered his final instructions. Ayeisha did her usual pre-match kit check, ensuring that all her goalkeeping equipment was in her bag.

Stepping onto the blue pitch, the team received the best of welcomes again from the screaming Irish supporters.

'This is amazing,' Chloe Watkins said, turning to look at Ayeisha with an astonished look on her face.

'It's unbelievable, Chloe,' Ayeisha agreed, dragging her large goalkeeper's bag behind her.

Standing on the pitch for 'Ireland's Call', Ayeisha thought of her mum, and of how much she missed her. She knew her mum would be proud of her, especially on a day like this.

The match started. In the first quarter, Ayeisha found herself under attack from the black-shirted Canadian forwards.

During a Canadian short corner, with her Captain, Katie Mullan, and Elena Tice helping to protect the goal, Ayeisha carefully crept two steps out from the goal line. Growing big, she planted her feet and raised her arms high to block the charging forwards. Running alongside her, Katie pounced, captured the ball and hit it away safely.

'Good play, Ireland,' Ayeisha called out.

Moments later, Ayeisha was shadowing another Canadian forward, who had run into the circle unmarked. Diving along the ground, she cleared the shot. Huge cheers erupted around Energia Park.

The second quarter was far quieter for the Irish keeper – that is, until the last few minutes.

Peering through her helmet, Ayeisha saw a Canadian forward strike the ball from just outside the circle. Travelling fast, it tipped an Irish player's foot and went into the goal. Still on the ground after diving to attempt to stop the shot, Ayeisha looked up at the umpire.

'No goal,' the umpire said, signalling for a short corner. Ayeisha let out a sigh of relief.

That was the last time in the game that the ball found itself in the back of either goal. When the full-time whistle blew, Ayeisha knew what was coming. When Ireland tried to qualify for the last Olympics, in Rio in 2016, they had lost to China in a penalty shoot-out.

'You know what to do, Ayeisha. We've studied the players together,' Nigel said reassuringly. Nigel Henderson, or Nidge to the team, was Ayeisha's goalkeeping coach.

'We believe in you, now go out there and show everyone why you are the best goalkeeper in the world,' he said, resting a hand on her shoulder.

'I'll do my best, Nidge,' she replied.

Crossing the pitch to her goal for the first penalty shot, a feeling of loneliness came over Ayeisha. She had always understood that goalkeepers were different to the rest of the team. Glancing back at her team, Ayeisha knew right away what she needed to do.

'Focus. This is what I do,' she told herself softly.

Stephanie Norlander of Canada was first up, and she was lightning quick. Ayeisha ran out from the goal, arriving at Stephanie's feet just as she was turning to show the Irish keeper her back. Ayeisha dived, but the ball flew over her stick and into the back of the goal. 1-0 to Canada.

Ayeisha stood at the side of the pitch to watch the first Irish penalty against the Canadian goalkeeper. She could watch the action better from here, and it was a short walk back into the goal when it was her turn again.

Gill Pinder was up first for Ireland. With each player having only eight seconds to score, Ayeisha knew that when Gill's shot hit off the goalie's leg guards, it was too late for Gill to score.

'Walk out slowly, Ayeisha,' Ayeisha chanted to herself.

She remembered from her notes to walk out just a few steps from her goal, as Amanda Woodcroft, the Canadian midfielder, had a habit of taking shots from far out. Seeing the Irish goalkeeper wasn't running, Woodcroft dashed at Ayeisha and tapped the ball between her legs. Ayeisha tried desperately to swivel around to reach it, but it was too late. The ball had dribbled into the goal. The scoreboard flickered. 2-0.

Ayeisha walked away, trying not to look up at the crowd. 'I can do this,' she told herself. Suddenly, the Irish fans were up on their feet – Ireland's number 22, Nicci Daly, had fired a shot past the Canadian keeper. 2-1.

Ayeisha's third penalty left her face-down on the ground after colliding with the Canadian Captain – she had fouled the player. Canada were awarded a chance to score from the penalty spot, with Ayeisha having to remain on her goal line until the shot was taken. As she dived to her right, the ball was pushed to the opposite side of the goal. 3-1 to Canada.

It stayed 3-1 after Ireland's Róisín Upton took longer than the eight seconds allowed to score. A horn blew to let her know that the countdown had ended.

Looking at her team all huddled together, Ayeisha felt the pressure building up inside of her. Another goal for Canada and Ireland's dream of going to the Olympics would be over.

Ayeisha saw Canada's number 23, Brie Stairs, arching over the ball. Brie liked to shoot near the goal. Racing fast out of the goals, she was toe-to-toe with Brie within seconds. Hand pads up, she covered the player like a blanket, forcing her to take the shot early. A roar went up from the stands as the ball went wide. The Green Army was not yet finished.

Ayeisha was kneeling down to adjust her leg guards when Beth Barr belted a shot under the diving Canadian keeper. 3-2. The noise in Energia Park was deafening.

Recognising the black sleeves of Shanlee Johnston, Ayeisha prepared herself for a high shot from the Canadian player. Johnston swung her stick high over-head, and her shot skyrocketed over Ayeisha, missing the goal completely.

'We can do this, we can do this,' Ayeisha repeated as she left the goal area.

Ayeisha watched from the sideline as Chloe Watkins danced with the Canadian keeper. The dance suddenly ended when Chloe hit a spectacular reverse shot that found the goal with ease. The Irish supporters could not be silenced. 3–3.

It was sudden death. The team that failed to score next would not be going to the Olympics.

The atmosphere was tense as Róisín volunteered to take the first shot for Ireland, hoping to find the goal within the allotted eight seconds. Ayeisha could not look as Róisín battled hard with the Canadian keeper. Just before the horn blew, she shot the ball across the goal, hitting the post and scoring. Róisín punched the air as the Irish supporters sang 'Go Green Army'. 4–3 to Ireland.

It was up to Ayeisha now. If she could stop Canada from scoring, Ireland would be on their way to Tokyo.

A tense silence fell over the pitch as Amanda Woodcroft stepped out to take the penalty for Canada. Woodcroft had been successful in scoring against Ayeisha earlier.

She ran out, and Ayeisha started counting down the eight seconds. Woodcroft spun around, nearly knocking Ayeisha off her feet. With only seconds to go, Woodcroft lifted her stick to shoot, but it only clipped the ball. Ayeisha dropped down into a split to block. In a desperate attempt to score, Woodcroft went around her and shot the ball up into the net.

But the horn had blown before the shot was even taken. It had taken longer than the eight seconds, and the Irish supporters were already celebrating.

The energy in the Energia Park was electric as the Irish team bounded across the pitch to embrace Ayeisha. They had done it – they had made history by becoming the first Irish female team to qualify for the Olympics.

CHAPTER 2

LARNE DAYS

'Race you to the top of Teletubby Hill,' Ayeisha yelled, running out of the house and leaping over Busker. Busker, the family dog, was far too busy drinking out of his favourite bowl to notice. It was another hot summer's day in Larne and the ice-cold water was so refreshing.

'That's not fair, you had a head start,' Seanna shouted.

Seanna, who lived next door, was Ayeisha's closest friend.

Ayeisha could still remember meeting Seanna for the first time, when Seanna's family had moved to Larne from Belfast. It was in Seanna's front garden and Ayeisha was holding her mum's hand.

'This is Seanna, say hi,' Ayeisha's mum said, tugging gently on Ayeisha's small hand.

'Hi Seanna, I'm Ayeisha,' she blurted out.

'Hi Esha,' Seanna timidly replied, staring down at the ground.

'No, silly-billy, it's: eye-ee-sha!' Ayeisha said very slowly.

'Sorry,' Seanna mumbled beginning to feel her face go red.

'That's okay; it takes a little bit of getting used to.

Do you want to see my brother's gerbils?' Ayeisha asked, grabbing Seanna's sleeve and pulling her away from the safety of the talking mums.

If Ayeisha was the chalk, then Seanna was the cheese.

Ayeisha could not sit still for one minute. 'An excitable chatterbox,' her teachers would say. She was forever dreaming up the next great big adventure for the two friends to go on – even if it meant getting them into trouble!

Seanna was quiet and shy, the sensible one of the two, and never wished to be the centre of attention. She was the type of best friend who would say: 'We can't do that,' or, 'It's late, we should go home.'

Across the road from where the McFerrans lived was Teletubby Hill, the meeting place for all the kids in the neighbourhood. On the top of the hill stood a single, towering tree. On a sunny day it was a welcome resting place to cool off underneath. At the far side of the hill stood a wall of great oak trees. Beyond this the hill suddenly gave way to a cliff, dropping down to the sea.

'Hang on, Ayeisha,' called Seanna as Ayeisha sped past.

'Hi, Seanna. You'll catch her if you go through Maguire's garden,' Reece, Ayeisha's brother said, kneeling on the step and oiling the chain on his BMX.

Ayeisha had two brothers, Reece and Shea, and an older sister called Tamara.

Reece, the older of the two brothers, liked nothing better than fixing things. He also loved taking things apart to see how they worked, or if he could make them work better! Their mum would be heard shouting about the house: 'Reece, what have you done now?' when the washing machine door would suddenly fly open and foamy suds would spill out onto the floor.

Shea, the youngest of the McFerran children, loved the outdoors. He was at home in the garden, jumping about in his bright yellow wellies. The garden shed was Shea's favourite place in the world. Its shelves were neatly stacked with pots; seeds in labelled bags hung from hooks; and shovels and rakes stood to attention in the corner. Shea took pride in ensuring 'his' shed was kept tidy.

Tamara, the eldest, was also the shyest in the family. Being the eldest, Tamara was seen as the responsible sibling. Tamara loved to read, and when she wasn't reading she would be up in her room studying for an important test. Their mum relied on Tamara to keep control when she was at work. This was mostly an easy task, as the boys would usually keep themselves busy, but Ayeisha? Well, Ayeisha's adventures could take her anywhere.

Seanna arrived at the top of Teletubby Hill to find a group of the neighbourhood kids stretched out in the dark shadows of the tree. Some of the older ones were sunbathing outside of the shade. Seanna could see that they were starting to turn a pinkish colour that they might regret later.

'Jodie, did you see Ayeisha?' Seanna asked.

Jodie lived a couple of doors down from Ayeisha and went to the same school.

'I sure did, she nearly stood on my head going up,' Jodie said, squinting out from between her fingers, the sun too bright for her to see who was standing over her.

'Up here, up here!' Ayeisha called out.

'I can't see you, Ayeisha,' Seanna said.

'Seanna, Seanna, I'm over here,' Ayeisha teased, realising her best friend still couldn't see her.

Twisting her head to hear where the voice was coming from, Seanna spotted Ayeisha's legs dangling high above.

'Be careful, you'll fall down,' Seanna said worriedly.

'I can see Scotland,' Ayeisha shouted, ignoring her friend's plea, and the faces of the sunbathers and shade-grabbers that were now staring up at her.

Ayeisha liked sitting alone in the tree. She knew it was too dangerous for any of the other kids to climb up into. From her perch, she watched the monstrous container ships criss-cross the Port of Larne. She wondered where they were going, and what faraway places they had been to.

Ayeisha had never been outside of Northern Ireland. She dreamed that someday she would go on a plane and visit distant places where people spoke different languages.

Other kids in her class would return after the summer holidays tanned, with bright bracelets up their arms. They would stand at the top of the class and tell tales of swimming in pools the size of car parks, or of golden beaches that stretched for miles. Some of her classmates had travelled to countries like America. Ayeisha was in awe of this. She had seen the Statue of Liberty and the Empire State building on TV and was amazed at how tall they were.

'Ayeisha, we're all leaving to play soccer,' Seanna called, beginning to get annoyed with her best friend.

Soccer was Seanna's only way to entice Ayeisha down.

'Last one there goes in goals,' Jodie screamed.

Seanna remained behind as the others ran away.

'Coming down right away, Seanna,' Ayeisha yelled, as she dropped from branch to branch like an acrobat.

Landing on the ground beside Seanna with a thump, Ayeisha beamed.

'Don't worry, Seanna, I'll go in goals,' she said.

CHAPTER 3

HOOKED

Ayeisha's mum, Sandra, was parking the car when a lady carrying a bunch of leaflets approached her window. Ayeisha, sitting in the back of the car was busy tying the football boots she had borrowed, without permission, from her brother's bedroom.

It was Sunday morning soccer at Moyle Primary.

Ayeisha enjoyed playing soccer. It didn't bother her that she was the only girl, as she was often picked first by the captain to play in a match.

'Hello, Sandra, how have you been?' the leaflet lady said cheerily, sticking her head into the open window of the car.

'Oh, I'm good thanks, Alice,' Sandra replied, startled.

'Sandra, we are hosting a free hockey practice this afternoon at Larne Ladies. It's for under-9s; I was wondering if Ayeisha would like to come along?' she asked, passing in a leaflet to Ayeisha.

'Can I go, Mum, please?' Ayeisha begged, staring at the colourful pictures on the leaflet. 'Look at the girls wearing the pretty red hockey skirts,' Ayeisha said eagerly, thrusting the leaflet into her mum's face.

'They are actually hockey skorts, Ayeisha. Underneath those skirts are shorts,' the leaflet lady said. Ayeisha giggled, having never heard of a 'skort' before.

'Okay, Ayeisha. I'll collect you after soccer and we'll go straight there,' her mum replied, glaring at her for laughing. 'Now, you'd better run along or you'll be late for soccer.' Ayeisha leaped out of the car. 'Thanks, Mum. Thank you, leaflet lady.'

'It's Mrs Kirby, Ayeisha,' her mum called after her.

Standing on the soccer pitch, Ayeisha wondered what hockey was all about. Ayeisha loved every type of sport – it didn't matter what it was, she was always up for trying it.

Most days and nights, the young 'Larnian' would be playing tennis, cricket or gymnastics, or swimming in the Larne Leisure Centre. Being next to the sea, swimming was a very popular pastime for the people of Larne. Lately, Ayeisha had even taken to practising her new judo moves out on her brother Reece.

'It's your turn in goals,' the captain of Moyle Primary said, handing Ayeisha a pair of mucky gloves.

Ayeisha had scored the only two goals of the match for her team, but this didn't matter. She was part of the team, and each of the other players had had their go in goals. It was 2-2, with only a few minutes left in the match.

'It's a draw – penalties!' the referee roared after blowing the final whistle, spinning to point at Ayeisha in the goal. As she had been the last keeper in goals, it was down to Ayeisha to save the shots.

A small boy, covered from head to toe in mud, arrived at the penalty spot. Ayeisha could only make out his beady, round eyes.

Stepping backwards, the boy rushed at the ball, kicking it to the left side of the goal. Ayeisha quickly sank into a spectacular leg split, her right foot stopping the ball from going into the net. The boys from her team cheered.

'Would you like to take our penalty?' the captain of her team asked, as he stuck out his hand to help her up.

'Okay,' said Ayeisha from the ground.

'Great! Get this goal and we win,' he said.

The referee placed the ball on the spot and nodded at Ayeisha. Without taking a single step, Ayeisha struck the ball, sending it high over the goalkeeper's head. 3-2. The boys from her team roared with delight. The parents who had stayed to watch clapped from the car park.

'Are you ready for hockey?' her mum asked, as Ayeisha skipped towards her.

'Sure am,' Ayeisha replied.

'You'll need to change those mucky boots before we get there,' her mum said. 'And they'd better be clean before you give them back to your brother. And Mrs Kirby said you should keep your shin guards on, you'll need them.'

When they arrived at Larne Ladies Hockey Club, Ayeisha saw some girls from her school gathered in front of the clubhouse. The leaflet lady was there too, but she was now dressed in a red-and-white tracksuit and had a hockey stick over her shoulder.

'I'll stay for a bit, Ayeisha, in case you don't like it,' her mum said as they walked up to the clubhouse.

'Of course I'll like it,' she replied. 'You go home and rest, Mum. I'll be fine.'

Ayeisha's mum had not been well lately and had to go to the hospital for a lot of appointments.

'Welcome, young ladies,' the leaflet lady said. 'My name is Alice Kirby and I am the under-9s hockey coach here at Larne Ladies Hockey Club.'

The girls all looked around at each other.

'Before we get started, I'd like to talk to you about the rules of hockey,' Coach Kirby continued, as she began to explain how the sport is played.

'So, if the ball touches my feet it's a foul?' Ayeisha questioned.

'Yes, this is not soccer. Your feet are only there in hockey to run with, unless you're the goalkeeper that is – the goalkeeper can kick the ball,' coach Kirby said.

'And you can't hit the ball in the air to another player?' Ayeisha asked, waving her hand high above her head.

'It's far too dangerous, especially at your age,' the coach replied, looking along the line of children to see if anyone else had questions.

Seeing that Ayeisha appeared disappointed, the coach said, 'Can anyone tell me how hockey is quite similar to soccer?'

'There are the same amount of players?' Ayeisha belted out.

'That's correct, well done, Ayeisha. There are eleven players on a team, including the goalkeeper, and what's more, the positions are the same,' the coach said, smiling approvingly.

Ayeisha was happy she'd got the question right.

'You will know that in most games played on a pitch, you have two halves of forty to forty-five minutes in length. However, in hockey, you have four quarters, each fifteen minutes or so long,' the coach announced.

'That's confusing,' the girl next to Ayeisha, in a white baseball cap, mumbled.

Coach Kirby had been leaning against a silver car during the entire talk. Laying her hockey stick on the roof of the car, she removed keys from her tracksuit pocket and opened the boot.

Peering in, the girls could see that it was filled to the brim with hockey sticks.

'If you would like to line up and pick out a stick, I will demonstrate how to hold a hockey stick,' she said.

Ayeisha found it difficult to get up fast, her legs now aching from doing the splits at soccer earlier.

Standing at the back of the line, she could see the different-coloured sticks being pulled out from the car. When it was finally her turn, she looked in and saw that the boot was empty.

'Mrs Kirby, there are none left,' she said gloomily.

'You can use my daughter's stick, Ayeisha,' the coach replied, opening the car door and handing her a bright pink-and-white hockey stick. 'With your left hand, grip the top of the stick. Then place your right hand down lower, wherever is most comfortable for you,' the coach demonstrated.

'Fabulous, girls,' said Coach Kirby as they all tried out the correct grip. 'Now, let's go out onto the hockey pitch. Anyone who doesn't have a gumshield can take one from here, they're new,' she continued, holding out a basket.

The pitch was different to any Ayeisha had ever played on. The grass was artificial – it didn't grow. It felt strange, but in a nice way – there were no brown puddles or mucky patches anywhere! The gumshield was strange too; it hurt Ayeisha's gums, but the coach had explained how hard the ball was, and that a knock could be serious.

'Pass the ball about; get a feel for it,' the coach said.

Ayeisha took her first steps as a hockey player, with the ball resting against the bottom of the stick. She then began to move faster, the ball staying close by.

'This is great,' she said, looking around and seeing the girl with the white baseball cap running beside her.

'Are you coming back next week?' the girl asked.

'I am; I love it!' Ayeisha answered, passing her the ball.

CHAPTER 4

HAPPY FEET

'Before you go, Ayeisha, will you play us a little ditty?' her granny asked, carrying a tray piled high with freshly baked scones.

'You can have the biggest one,' she said, smiling at the tray, hoping that this would bribe her grand-daughter into playing something.

'Deal,' Ayeisha replied, reaching down for the rectangular case.

Carefully removing the flute, Ayeisha put it together and placed her lips to one end.

The sitting room fell silent.

Ayeisha played beautifully, head tilted slightly to one side, her eyes closed throughout the entire tune. When she had finished, she delicately returned the flute to the safe haven of its case.

Her granddad sat up proudly in his favourite chair in the corner. Behind him were shelves of old Irish records, along with trophies and medals.

'You are so good. Isn't she, Jimmy?' her granny said, thrusting the tray under Ayeisha's nose.

'She gets her talent from me,' her granddad boasted, leaning forward to steal the biggest scone away from his granddaughter.

'Too slow, Granda,' Ayeisha said, snatching it from his grasp.

'She must get her speed from me then,' her granny laughed, sitting down on the armrest of her husband Jimmy's chair.

Ayeisha's grandparents lived only a ten-minute drive away from her house. Ayeisha would go there often to listen to Irish music and watch video recordings on the TV of her granddad singing on stage. During the breaks in the TV show, a team of Irish dancers would come out and entertain the audience.

Ayeisha loved the costumes and hair of the young performers, but it was the speedy footwork of the dancers that grabbed her attention most.

'Are you ready for your competition later, Ayeisha?'

her granddad asked, passing her the butter dish for her second scone.

'Granda Jimmy, if I win, Mum is going to buy me my own phone,' Ayeisha said eagerly.

'A phone? What would you want with one of those things?' he scoffed.

'To talk to my friends and play games,' she replied.

'But you can do all of that without a phone,' her granddad said, looking a bit confused.

'Tell you what, will you just bring your granddad back another trophy for the shelf?' he said, with his arms opened wide, waiting for a hug.

'Ready, Ayeisha? It's a long drive and we've got to do your hair when we get there,' her mum said, standing in the doorway.

'Have you got everything, Sandra?' her granny asked from the armrest.

'I have, Mona, I picked up the dress this morning from the seamstress. She did a good job.'

Ayeisha enjoyed travelling to Irish dancing competitions alone with her mum. They would talk about almost anything on their trip – how many sheep were in a field they just passed; how hockey training was going; who could spot a car from across the border;

favourite songs; places they'd like to visit in the world – Ayeisha's answer to this was always the same: Disneyland in Paris, France. Her mum would say, 'Someday, Ayeisha, we'll all go there together.'

Arriving at the venue for the competition, Ayeisha recognised Caitlin and Karen from her Irish dancing school. Karen's hair was made up into tight ringlets, and Caitlin was wearing the new dress she had been talking about in class that week. It had a golden harp on the front, and frilly white lace around the neck and at the bottom of the sleeves.

'Mum, look at Karen's hair! She went to a proper hairdresser yesterday. And Caitlin's dress is so pretty – it was bought by her aunt in England from an expensive shop in London.' Ayeisha looked on enviously.

'Ayeisha, all of that doesn't matter. You just go out there and do your best. And remember to enjoy yourself, that's what's really important,' her mum said affectionately.

The dressing room was a noisy place to get changed in. On entering, you were met with a cloud of hairspray that stung your eyes. Hassled mums jostled with one another to find precious space. Hairbrushes and make-up palettes were flung about the room. Older sisters stood on guard in front of rows of expensive costumes. Girls who had completed the transformation into Irish dancing princesses were being hauled up against a wall for photos.

'Stand still, mind your dress, don't touch your hair … now, smile!' the mums would roar over the traditional music blaring from the stage.

'Over here, Ayeisha,' her mum called out, holding up Ayeisha's costume like a banner to get her attention.

'Nice spot, Mum,' Ayeisha said, sitting down on the small chair.

'We don't have long,' her mum said, pulling a curling tongs from her handbag and plugging it into the last available socket.

'Let's get this on you first,' she said, tearing away the plastic covering the dress.

The sleeveless, burgundy velvet dress had Celtic designs stitched between the pleats. It had previously been Tamara's, and it had been altered quite a few times already over the years. Ayeisha didn't mind wearing it. She would say it was her 'trophy dress'. Her granddad said it was 'old-fashioned', and that the judges liked that.

Ayeisha also wore a delicate silk shirt and poodle-white socks. The only item of her own was her shoes, or 'ghillies' as they are called – like ballet shoes, but with laces.

'Arms up, Ayeisha,' her mum said, dropping the dress over her head.

'Ten minutes for the Lisa Dempsey School of Dancing,' a male voice bellowed over the intercom. This was Ayeisha's Irish dancing school in Larne.

'Hurry, Ayeisha, we have to do your hair yet,' her mum said, grabbing a clump of her hair and wrapping it around the hot curlers.

Stepping around Ayeisha from foot to foot, as if she too was doing an Irish jig, her mum plunged the curlers in and out of Ayeisha's hair.

'Can I borrow your hairspray?' Ayeisha's mum asked a frantic-looking mum who was quizzing her daughter about a missing headband. Without waiting for a response, she snatched up the can of hairspray.

'Close your eyes,' she said, as the can released a sticky mist that Ayeisha felt fall all over her.

'Final call for the Lisa Dempsey School of Dancing,' came the announcement.

'Go, go! I'll be out front watching, but I'll meet you back here afterwards,' her mum said, pushing Ayeisha through the crowded room. 'And enjoy it!' she called out, as Ayeisha disappeared through the door.

Ayeisha was the last dancer to take to the stage. Arms straight by her sides, she readied herself for the first note. When it came, she leaped high up into the air, landing perfectly, arms glued to her sides.

Her feet moved very fast, her steps matching every beat. She spun several times, kicking out as she did, her legs flying far above her waist.

Ayeisha was enjoying it so much that she didn't hear the audience clapping every time she jumped. With her chin up and eyes fixed on the back of the packed room, Ayeisha counted to herself as she flicked her feet in and out. Her mum smiled up at her, her warm face framed by her beautiful red hair.

With her hands on her waist, Ayeisha finished her set with a final twirl, the pleats of her burgundy dress taking flight.

Facing the crowd, she nodded before walking to the side of the stage to wait for the results among the other young dancers.

The dressing room was full to the brim with dancers, parents, relatives and teachers when Ayeisha entered. Seeing her mum in the crowd, she rushed towards her.

'You should call your granddad,' her mum said as she hugged her tight.

'Granddad, it's Ayeisha, I won!' she screamed over the racket in the room.

'And Granddad, I'm ringing you from my new phone.'

CHAPTER 5

KIT UP!

'But Mum, I really like their cool purple uniform,' Ayeisha pleaded.

'Ayeisha, you are only eleven years old. You would have to walk for fifteen minutes alone through the estate to catch the 7.30am bus to the private school,' her mum said softly.

'Please, Mum, I promise I'll get up early. I'll even make everyone's breakfast before I leave,' said Ayeisha.

'Your sister Tamara goes to Larne Grammar School, and she loves it.'

'Yes, but Tamara loves doing homework, and she gets loads,' Ayeisha argued.

'I just don't have the money to send you there, Ayeisha. Anyway, why do you want to go there so much?

You know they don't play hockey at that school?' said her mum, turning away to switch on the radio.

Ayeisha thought that everybody played hockey in Larne, especially in school. The colour of the uniform now no longer mattered.

'Okay so, I'll go to Larne Grammar School, but I'll need a new hockey stick,' Ayeisha replied cheekily, unsure if her demand for a new stick could be heard over the fiddle music on the radio.

Larne Grammar School was one of the biggest schools in Larne.

It took very fit legs to travel up the steep hill to the school's main gate. It was a friendly place, and Ayeisha soon discovered that she enjoyed going there.

Ayeisha's favourite subjects at the Grammar were Art and History, though she wasn't very good at remembering dates, which is quite important for History!

Her Art class was at the back of the school, in the new, modern extension. Art was on a Friday, when everybody in her class was always in a good mood, including her Art teacher, Mrs Farrell.

Today was no different to any other Friday.

Mrs Farrell allowed the class to listen to music while she went around handing out chocolates.

She would stop by each desk and say the same thing: 'Lovely work, keep it up.' As long as you had a brush or pencil in hand and were making an effort, Mrs Farrell was happy.

Ayeisha liked the relaxed atmosphere, though she knew Mrs Farrell could get cross easily if you were talking to the person next to you, or if your work was not completed before the end-of-class bell rang out.

From her desk, Ayeisha could see the school's hockey pitch. She stared out the window, smiling. After Art class was lunch, and after lunch was double PE – and PE meant one thing: hockey.

'Ayeisha McFerran, stop daydreaming!' Mrs Farrell shouted from the top of the class. 'If you keep it up, I'll move you up beside me.'

Ayeisha jolted in her seat, smudging her charcoal drawing of a hockey player scoring a goal.

'I think you've made it look better, Ayeisha,' Barry chuckled next to her.

'Go away, Barry,' she muttered, afraid to look down at the mess she had caused.

'You've made the ball look like it's flying through the air, see? The smudge lines behind the ball,' he said, pointing at the picture.

'Very clever, Ayeisha, lovely work,' her teacher said, now standing next to her. 'You must look out the window more often,' she whispered, just as the school bell rang.

The school locker room was a cold place to get changed in. But there was great excitement amongst the girls, which seemed to heat up the room. Loud chatter and laughter echoed under the low ceiling.

'Throw me over a gumshield, Ruth,' Ayeisha called out.

Ruth Maguire was the team captain and one of Ayeisha's closest friends.

Grabbing the gumshield, Ruth flung it fast at Ayeisha across the room. Ayeisha, seeing her friend was up to no good, leapt to her feet, catching the gumshield with her open hand.

'Good catch, Ayeisha,' Ruth shouted over.

Shaking her head, Ayeisha reached down into her sports bag to find her shin guards.

'I'm looking for a volunteer,' came a roar from outside of the dressing room. It was Miss Parker, the school hockey coach and PE teacher.

'I need a goalkeeper; who would like to try out?'

Ayeisha only heard, 'Who would like to try out?'

She darted out of the locker room, screaming, 'Pick me, pick me!'

'That's great, Ayeisha, let's get the gear,' her coach replied.

'But coach, I have my gear. Look: stick, shin guards, gumshield.'

'You'll need more than that, Ayeisha,' her coach winked, strolling away from her.

'I've never been in here before,' Ayeisha said, standing in the middle of a windowless room. Rows of shelves held bulging bags of sports equipment. On one side, Ayeisha noticed labels marked 'rugby'.

'Take this and we'll see how it fits,' Coach Parker said tugging a large bag down from the opposite shelf. It was long and wide, and made a thud as it landed by Ayeisha's feet.

'What is it?' Ayeisha asked, staring nervously at it.

'A goalie kit,' her coach said, as if it were obvious. 'Take a look.'

Unzipping the bag, Ayeisha was greeted by a smell of damp. Inside were two oversized yellow foam leg guards, two giant black soft shoes called kickers, a chest guard, padded shorts, and two odd-looking yellow hand protectors, one flat and the other with a hole in it.

Ayeisha was speechless. She had only seen goal-keepers in their full kit at Larne Ladies, and they were much older than her.

'Of course you'll need a helmet too. This one should do,' Coach Parker said, grabbing a battered yellow helmet with black grills across the front.

'Let's go, Ayeisha. I think it has wheels, so you can pull it behind you.'

It was a long walk back to the hockey pitch, and dragging the goalie kit made the journey even longer. As Ayeisha arrived pitchside, she could hear some of her teammates snigger. Ayeisha felt awkward. She dropped the kit bag and began shoving it away with her foot.

'Ayeisha, you can put on your kit now,' her coach said loudly.

'Can I help her, Miss Parker?' Ruth asked, turning to glare disapprovingly at the rest of the team gathered on the bench.

'Of course, Ruth, thank you. It's best to lay all the kit out first.'

By the time the bag was empty, it looked as though a scary foamy monster was lying flat on its back.

'I never realised how much kit a goalkeeper wore,' Ayeisha said, looking surprised.

'Let's start with those yellow leg guards,' Ruth replied, going behind Ayeisha and clipping them on.

'Put this over your head. Gosh, it smells, Ayeisha,' Ruth said, handing Ayeisha the chest protector.

'Pass me those kicker slipper things,' Ayeisha said, beginning to enjoy being dressed.

'You look like a Transformer,' Ruth said, trying hard not to laugh.

'Bumblebee,' Ayeisha answered, suddenly spotting the shorts on the ground. 'We forgot the padded shorts, Ruth,' she said in a panic.

'I think you can pull them up over the kickers,' Ruth replied, picking up the shorts and sitting down next to Ayeisha's feet. 'Lift your leg,' she demanded.

Balancing on one leg, Ayeisha offered Ruth her foot, as Ruth slid the shorts carefully over the kicker. Its strap caught in the waistband of the shorts, sending Ayeisha tumbling backwards.

Both friends rolled about, laughing hysterically on the ground.

'Thank you, Ruth, I'll finish up here. You can go and warm up with the rest of the team,' Coach Parker said, standing over them.

'Bye bye, Bumblebee, see you out there,' Ruth hollered as she jumped up.

'Put on the helmet, Ayeisha, and don't forget the hand protectors,' Coach Parker said.

Standing in the goal, Ayeisha looked over at the rest of her team, at the other end of the pitch. She loved playing hockey with her friends, but now she felt alone. The sides of her head were hurting from the helmet.

'Pay attention, Ayeisha,' Coach Parker called. 'I'll hit some balls at you, and you try to kick them away. Don't worry if some of them get past you.' Coach Parker raised her hockey stick to take the first shot against the Grammar's newest goalkeeper.

As the first ball came near Ayeisha's foot, she kicked it so hard it went out to the middle of the pitch, where her friends were gathered. The team turned to look at what was happening.

Ayeisha was well used to kicking a ball, since she played soccer with Moyle Primary.

'Now try the side of your foot, Ayeisha,' the coach yelled.

Striking with the side of her foot, Ayeisha sent the

ball flying in different directions. Shouts went up
from her team. Ayeisha grinned proudly.

'You are a natural, Ayeisha,' her coach called out. 'A
natural!'

CHAPTER 6

FIRST MATCH

Acloud of dust rose up in the Grammar car park as the previous year's under-12s hockey champions arrived. Rows of young, eager faces stared out of the large windows on the side of the bus.

Larne Grammar were already down on the pitch warming up. It was 10am, a typical Spring Saturday morning in Larne, and the champions from Belfast were early.

Ayeisha was by the side of the gravel pitch laying out her goalie gear, while the rest of the team did hockey drills out on the pitch. This would be Ayeisha's first match as goalkeeper. She was very excited about that, but she did miss playing outfield with her friends.

At training over the past few weeks, she had mislaid the key to the equipment closet several times 'by mistake', to avoid going in goals. The school caretaker came to the rescue each time however, flourishing a spare key like he was pulling a rabbit out of a magician's hat.

'Thank you, Mr Gibbons, again. You're a star,' Coach Parker could be heard saying loudly from the dugout.

'Ayeisha, Mr Gibbons has found a spare key. Can you run up and get your gear?' she would shout at Ayeisha, who was concentrating on passing the ball to her teammates on the far side of the pitch.

'By the time I get there, come back, and put on the gear, Miss, training will be nearly over,' Ayeisha would protest.

'You need the practice, Ayeisha, and putting on the gear correctly is so important,' the coach would insist.

It wasn't so much being the goalkeeper that bothered Ayeisha, though she did at times look enviously at her team running about the pitch while she stood alone in goals. It was the before and after parts that she didn't like so much.

Ayeisha would have to put on and take off the goalie gear by herself. This took quite some time. And then there was the long walk to the equipment closet to put the kit back in its place. By the time Ayeisha returned, the team would often have all gone home.

Today being a Saturday, Mr Gibbons the caretaker was not at school, so Ayeisha had to bring the kit home with her after the match. This meant she couldn't go into town with her friends later, which made her feel a little sad and left out.

'Hey, are you in this team, goalie?' screamed Coach Parker, standing in the middle of the team huddle on the halfway line. Grabbing her helmet, Ayeisha waddled over as fast as she could in her heavy goalie gear and stood awkwardly outside of the huddle.

'Move over, Kerry, and let Ayeisha in,' Ruth called from the other side of the huddle, interrupting the coach's instructions for the match.

'Sorry, Ayeisha, I didn't see you there' Kerry said, playfully grabbing Ayeisha's hand pad and pulling her into the huddle.

'Girls, pay attention,' said Coach Parker. 'Belfast like to send all their midfield players up along with their forwards when they've got the ball. So defence need to get back fast and support Ayeisha.' Her voice had dropped to a whisper, seeing Belfast assemble nearby.

'Ruth, do you have anything to add?' the coach said, turning to the captain.

'Everyone be sure to mark up, and cover behind Ayeisha if they take the ball out to the side of the goal,' she ordered.

'Goalie, would you like to say something?' the coach asked, looking over at Ayeisha.

Ayeisha shook her head, the sides of the helmet digging into her head with each shake. She hadn't decided yet whether she liked being called 'Goalie'.

'Larne, Larne, Larne, Larne …' the players began to chant softly, getting steadily louder until a chorus of screams belted out. Then the Grammar hockey team dispersed to take up their positions on the pitch.

'Goalkeeper ready?' called out the umpire, pointing at Ayeisha. Hitting the top of the goalpost with her stick was Ayeisha's own special way of saying 'Yes'.

The whistle blew to start the match. Within seconds, Ayeisha was running out of her goal, her leg guards stopping a shot and sending the ball out to a Larne player, who raced away with it up the pitch.

Ayeisha took a deep breath. 'Phew, that was a close one,' she whispered.

The action was now at the other end of the pitch.
Ayeisha was happy with the break. It gave her a chance
to watch her team try to score against the visitors.

'Out to Emily, she's free!' Ayeisha screamed,
pointing with her stick at Emily Wright, the team's
best forward. Her voice sounded very strange in
the helmet. Hearing the shout, Emily received the
ball and pushed it between the legs of the other
goalkeeper.

Cheers went up from the Larne crowd, standing on
the hillside nearby. 1-0.

Now Belfast were back on the centre line, tipping
off faster than Larne had expected.

'Mark up, mark up,' Ayeisha pleaded.

Watching closely as the Belfast players passed to
one another, Ayeisha became dizzy, her helmet not
helping as it continued to press in on the sides of
her head. A line of bright white Belfast shirts quickly
came into view.

Ayeisha rushed out to the penalty spot and slid
sideways on the ground. The unforgiving sharp gravel
tore into her knee as Ayeisha's feet met with the ball,
sending it away. The blonde Belfast forward had no
time to stop, and tumbled over Ayeisha.

Rising to her feet, the angry Belfast player slyly flicked loose gravel into Ayeisha's face. Ayeisha's whole body ached as she lay on the ground. She didn't hear the half-time whistle blow and could barely make out Ruth's orange hockey shoes standing by her head.

'Are you going to get up soon, Ayeisha?' Ruth sniggered, reaching down to help her friend. 'By the way, great save. If you keep that up, you'll never play outfield again.'

Ayeisha reversed into her goal and sat down on the backboard, glad of the rest, but trembling with excitement.

Her teammates arrived and squashed in on either side of her.

Ayeisha didn't remove her helmet as Coach Parker, sitting in the goal, gave feedback on their playing.

'Goalie, you are doing a great job,' Coach Parker smiled over at her.

The rest of the game was far quieter. The two teams were fighting over the ball at midfield, neither able to break away. Ruth, as usual, was at the centre of it all.

Ayeisha suddenly saw the Belfast army charging at her, led by their captain, number nine.

'Watch number nine,' Ayeisha shouted. Entering the goal area, or circle – which is actually shaped like a large capital D – number nine hit the ball hard. It rocketed towards the top corner of the net. Like a starfish, Ayeisha stretched out, tipping the ball safely over the crossbar with her stick. It trembled, sending shivers up her arm that felt like pins and needles.

'Well done, goalie,' Coach Parker screamed from the dugout. The crowd on the hill began to chant: 'Goalie, goalie,' as the full-time whistle blew. Ayeisha was glad she was wearing her helmet, as she could feel her cheeks begin to glow red.

In the middle of the pitch, her team were all hugging. There was little chance of Ayeisha joining them – weighed down by her gear, the celebrations would be over by the time she got there.

'Ayeisha, I'm the coach from Belfast,' a male voice bellowed as Ayeisha painfully removed her helmet.

'You were amazing – I can see you playing for Ulster someday,' he said, turning away to shake the hand of a beaming Coach Parker.

Behind the coach, Ayeisha spied a familiar figure at the railings at the side of the pitch. It was her mum. Running towards her, Ayeisha noticed that she appeared thinner.

'Mum, we won, and I saved so many!' she said breathlessly.

'I know, Ayeisha, I saw it all. You were fantastic,' her mum replied. 'Would you like to celebrate with your friends in town? I can take your goalie kit bag home for you.'

'Mum, I'd like to spend the day with you,' Ayeisha said. 'And did I tell you what the Belfast coach said to me?'

'No, Goalie, you didn't,' said her mum, smiling widely.

CHAPTER 7

HELPING HAND

'Ayeisha, where are you?' her mum asked softly.

'I'm out with my team in town, Mum,' she replied excitedly. 'We're just going into Subway for some food.' 'Can you please come home right away?' her mum responded.

'But Mum, it was our last hockey practice today. We'd planned the trip into town ages ago,' Ayeisha said.

'I'm really sorry, Ayeisha, but I need you home now,' her mum said. 'There's someone here who wants to meet you.'

Ayeisha was not happy. It wasn't easy to drag the school goalie kit bag through the centre of Larne.

She quickly lost count of the number of times she had to say 'Sorry', as the wheels ran over people's feet.

Arriving at the driveway to her house, Ayeisha saw a white car she didn't recognise. On its window was a sticker of a smiling daisy with the words 'Cancer Fund for Children'.

She came around to the back door, and spotted her mum standing at the kitchen sink, pouring water into the kettle. Everything seemed normal, except that Mum's usual country music wasn't blaring out through the window.

Ayeisha unlocked the garden shed and rolled the goalie kit bag into the corner, careful not to knock over any of Shea's gardening tools.

A man she had never seen before came out of the kitchen. 'Hi Ayeisha, I'm Gareth. How was hockey practice?' he asked. 'Your mum tells me you're a great goalkeeper.'

Puzzled, Ayeisha didn't reply, but smiled suspiciously at the man. She went into the kitchen, dropping her hockey shoes onto the mat with a thud.

On the kitchen table Ayeisha spied leaflets, pens and key rings with the same daisy face she had seen stuck on the car.

'Sorry about Subway, Ayeisha,' her mum said. 'Gareth called by to talk to you about how he helps families like ours.'

'Like ours? What do you mean, Mum?' Ayeisha quizzed.

'Ayeisha, when a family member has cancer, we try to offer the family a helping hand,' Gareth said, looking caringly towards Ayeisha's mum.

Ayeisha knew her mum frequently felt unwell, but she had never heard the word 'cancer' said out loud in their home before.

She didn't like hearing that her mum was sick, especially from someone she didn't know. Her mum never really spoke about her illness. There were days when her mum had loads of energy, but there were others when she struggled to get out of bed. She was a strong woman, who Ayeisha loved and admired very much.

'Can I have a key ring too?' Shea asked, bounding into the kitchen and clutching one of the daisy pens in his hand.

'Of course, Shea,' Gareth replied, handing Shea a bunch of key rings. Ayeisha wasn't surprised that Shea liked the floral design, being a big fan of gardening.

'Shea, Ayeisha, would you like to go bowling in Belfast next week? We can go to Subway afterwards,' Gareth said eagerly.

'That sounds great, Gareth. They would love that,' their mum said.

'We have a youth group called the Young Shoulders, and we do all sorts of activities. We even go away on camps,' he told them.

'Can Reece and Tamara come along too?' Ayeisha asked.

'Of course, Ayeisha,' Gareth replied, as he gathered up the leaflets into a neat pile. 'I'll call your mum and we can arrange it.'

'I just remembered that Ayeisha has a very important competition next weekend in Offaly,' her mum said regretfully.

'No problem at all, Sandra, we host activities every few weeks,' Gareth answered, handing Ayeisha a leaflet as he picked up his car keys to go.

The leaflet said 'Daisy News' in big yellow letters across the top, above a picture of a mum surrounded by her kids. Inside the leaflet was a story about a girl around Ayeisha's age who took care of her mum.

'Is it a hockey match in Offaly, Ayeisha?' Gareth asked, stepping out the back door.

'It's the All-Ireland Schools Javelin competition,' she replied nicely, thankful to Gareth for visiting.

With the hockey season coming to an end, Ayeisha had been doing a lot of athletics in school over the past few months. She had become very interested in the javelin.

'Wow, that's amazing, Ayeisha,' he called back as he passed by the kitchen window.

The next morning, Ayeisha set her alarm for 7am.

She had written a list of all the chores she would do around the house, starting with breakfast in bed for Mum.

Knocking quietly on her mum's bedroom door, she tiptoed in and placed down a tray with tea, toast and jam on the bedside locker. Gently rubbing her mum's shoulder, she whispered, 'Mum, breakfast is ready.'

The rest of the house was soon awoken to the sound of the hoover, as Ayeisha tore in and out of rooms, sucking up everything in her path. She liked hoovering – it felt a bit like hockey, stretching out as far as she could to reach an invisible ball.

Yelling into her brothers' bedroom, she ordered them to place any dirty clothes into the empty linen basket outside their door. It had rained the whole week, so Shea's clothes would be covered in muck from the garden. And the oil stains from Reece's BMX would no doubt take a second wash to remove.

She went cautiously down the stairs, unable to see over the full linen basket. As she landed in the hallway, she heard a familiar sound – loud music coming from the kitchen. Opening the door, her mum grabbed Ayeisha and took her in her arms, knocking the clothes everywhere.

'Thank you so much for breakfast, Ayeisha, and for helping with the chores,' her mum said, squeezing her tightly.

'Would you like me to show you how to make rice pudding?' her mum asked excitedly.

'Only if we can have some later, after our lunch,' Ayeisha said.

After dividing the rice pudding up into bowls to cool, the whole family went out to the garden.

Mum and Shea got busy gardening; Reece organised his tool kit; and Tamara sat on the back step reading a book. Ayeisha put on her school hockey goalie kit and dribbled a ball around a row of potted plants.

Ayeisha then made everyone lunch. Her mum requested only a small bowl of salad. 'Doctor's orders,' she said, as she picked glumly at the leaves.

'If you don't finish your rabbit food, Mum, then there's no rice pudding for you,' Ayeisha laughed.

In the days after Gareth's visit, Ayeisha woke early every morning to do chores and to make her mum breakfast, even on the day of the All Ireland Schools Javelin competition.

It was over a three-hour drive to Offaly from Larne. Ayeisha and her mum played all their favourite car games on the way.

Arriving into Tullamore Harriers Stadium, Ayeisha began to feel excited. She liked the javelin. It made her feel powerful.

Standing like a warrior with javelin in hand, she heard her school and name being announced on the stadium speakers. Ayeisha was the last to throw, but that didn't make her feel nervous. In fact, she preferred going last, as she could see how far the other athletes had thrown.

A loud cheer went up from behind a tall fence as she stepped up to the line. Ayeisha waited for the flag to drop before starting her run.

Tilting the javelin back behind her head, she let go suddenly, sending the long rod high up into the air. It wobbled slightly at first, before flying straight. Ayeisha could only watch as it went higher and further away. It was a really good throw.

The javelin shot down, its tip piercing the grass. In the distance, Ayeisha watched as a young woman with a measuring tape bent down to measure the throw. She spoke into a microphone, telling the announcer the distance she'd thrown. Ayeisha waited patiently.

Hearing the third and second places being announced over the speakers, Ayeisha knew she had won the All-Ireland Schools Javelin competition. She ran in the direction of the cheer. Her mum was jumping up and down, shouting her name. Ayeisha was thrilled that her mum was there to see her win.

On the drive back home to Larne, Ayeisha wore her All-Ireland medal around her neck. It was a very special day – and her mum beside her, beaming with pride, made it even better.

LIFE IS A ROLLERCOASTER

'It hurts so much,' Ayeisha cried out, resting her ear on her sister Tamara's shoulder.

Their mum was sitting in the seat across the aisle from them. Through her tears, Ayeisha could see her mum reach above her and press a small square button that lit up.

'Take a sip of this – the swallowing will help,' an air hostess said, passing a plastic cup to Ayeisha.

'Thank you,' Tamara replied, her sister far too upset to answer for herself.

Reece and Shea were sitting in the row behind, feeling uneasy at the attention their sister was attracting.

'Look, Ayeisha, I can see the Eiffel Tower!' Tamara said, trying to distract her from the pain.

It was Ayeisha's first time on a plane. None of her friends had warned her that you could get sore ears from flying. It was something to do with the plane flying up high and then coming back down quickly. She had climbed trees as tall as houses back on Teletubby Hill and her ears had never been sore.

Ayeisha had been counting the days until their family holiday to Disneyland Paris since being told about it.

A kind-faced man had been in their sitting room when Ayeisha got back in from school one day. A plate of the good visitor biscuits was on his lap, and Mum's favourite mug was in the man's hand.

'I'm speechless,' her mum was saying over and over again, as a puzzled Ayeisha came into the room. Reece and Shea were sitting on the floor with their mouths wide open. Tamara was standing by the fireplace, shaking her head and looking like she'd seen a ghost.

'Sit down, Ayeisha,' her mum said politely. 'I've something to tell you.'

Ayeisha didn't like the sound of this. Was it more bad news? The McFerrans had had their fair share of bad news lately.

'We are going to Disneyland Paris!' her mum screamed, startling the children. This was the most lively their mum had been for quite some time, and they were all thrilled to see it.

Ayeisha shot out of her chair and danced about the room with pure excitement, cautiously avoiding her brother's outstretched legs. She didn't care that a stranger was watching. Her brothers debated what they would bring on the holiday, and wondered if there would be bunk beds in the hotel. Tamara looked dreamily at her mum, saying, 'Oh, Mum, we can visit museums too.'

'The rides, the rides!' Ayeisha yelled into each of their faces, as if she was the only one with the sense to realise what going to Disneyland actually meant.

'I'll let you be with your family to enjoy the good news, Sandra,' the man said, rising to his feet and carefully handing the plate of biscuits to Tamara.

'Thank you again, this means so much to us,' her mum said as she opened the front door to let the man leave.

Tamara watched from the sitting room window as the man walked up the road. The man had no car. He was a local singer, a man from the neighbourhood, who had raised money for the McFerrans to go on a family holiday together – a holiday they would never forget.

The plane bounced along the runway. Untying her seatbelt, Ayeisha knelt up in her chair to tell her brothers that the pain in her ears had disappeared.

'Young lady, the seatbelt sign is still on. Please sit down,' a cross air hostess commanded.

'But we're not in the sky anymore.' Ayeisha was confused.

'It's her first time on a plane,' Tamara interrupted, tugging at Ayeisha's T-shirt.

'Sometimes the plane has to take off again pet, or the pilot may even have to swerve suddenly if something gets in the way,' the air hostess said nicely.

'Like a rollercoaster,' Ayeisha said quickly.

'Exactly,' she replied. 'Like at Disneyland,' the air hostess winked.

They arrived at their hotel. 'I'm on top,' Reece screeched, pushing past his younger brother and throwing his case up on the top bunk.

'You can take it in turns, boys,' their mum said, trying to calm the situation.

Ayeisha was sharing a room with Tamara and her mum.

She didn't care where she slept. She was planning to spend her days in the park on the rides, and her evenings in the hotel swimming pool.

'Wow, we're actually here,' Ayeisha said, as they walked through the colourful entrance to Disneyland Paris.

'Everybody has their passes, and here is some pocket money. Remember, it's to last you the whole day,' their mum said sternly. 'And Tamara, don't let Ayeisha out of your sight.'

'Be smart and be safe, kids,' she added. 'I will meet you back at the food court for lunch.'

'Bye, Mum,' Ayeisha replied, yanking at her sister's arm and running off.

It was spellbinding. Streets filled with beautiful buildings, steam trains choo-chooing by, vintage cars put-putting along, gift shops filled to the brim with Mickey Mouse delights, and giant, waving Disney characters, shaking hands with anyone who came near.

'Look, Tamara, there's Buzz Lightyear and Woody from *Toy Story*,' Ayeisha said, dragging her sister towards them.

'Come on, Ayeisha, I thought you wanted to go on some rides,' her sister answered, pulling her back.

'The hotel receptionist said that the queue for Crush's Coaster can be quite long, so we'd better hurry.'

They arrived at the line for the spinning roller-coaster, spotting Reece and Shea further ahead in the queue. Crush's Coaster was based on one of Ayeisha's favourite movies, *Finding Nemo*.

'Tamara, let's skip the queue and go up to the boys. We can pretend you were taking me to the toilet,' Ayeisha whispered.

Hearing his name being called somewhere off in the distance, Reece turned around to see his sisters passing out the queue. Something about 'toilet' and '*merci*' was being said. Tamara was the best in her class at French and she was keen to practise a few words on the holiday. It was working well, as obliging families moved out of their way.

'Ayeisha, you can sit facing forward in the front with Shea,' Tamara said as they all climbed into a large tortoise shell with four seats.

'I'm not sure I want to go now,' Shea said timidly, as the shell began to move off slowly along the track.

'Too late,' Ayeisha joked, elbowing her brother.

The rollercoaster ride zipped through dark, winding tunnels, spinning as it went around corners.

Shea gripped Ayeisha's hand tightly as each spin turned them both backwards. The *Finding Nemo* movie stars flashed up on the walls, chanting for the shell to go faster and faster. Blue and green lights ricocheted off the shell, falling like waves in front of their path. Ayeisha howled with glee. Her brother screamed with terror.

'That was amazing! I'm going again,' Ayeisha said as she watched Reece put his arm around a pale-looking Shea.

'You certainly are the daredevil of our family,' Tamara said teasingly.

'I know, I'm not afraid of anything,' Ayeisha replied.

'There'll be plenty of time to go again, Ayeisha. Let's all go now and spend some time with Mum. *D'accord?*' her sister said in a very grown-up French accent.

'Okay,' Ayeisha giggled, impressed by her sister's grasp of the local language, and pleased with herself for understanding that the word meant 'okay'.

'If we get the steam train, we'll be back faster,' she said.

CHAPTER 9

GOODBYE, MUM

'So that's Ayeisha McFerran,' Lee said, as he watched the fourteen-year-old goalkeeper fend off another shot.

'That's her all right,' Coach Parker said, her eyes closely fixed on Larne Grammar School's first match of the season.

Lee Young was the new under-16s Head Hockey Coach for Ulster. Ayeisha had been attending Ulster Hockey talent sessions during the summer, but had had to drop out as her mum was very sick.

Lee had heard great things about Ayeisha from the other Ulster coaches.

'Emma, do you think Ayeisha would be interested in coming for trials for the Ulster under-16s?' he asked.

'I think she would love that, Lee,' Coach Parker replied.

'Good, I'll let you know when they are on. Ayeisha is bound to know some of the other players at the Ulster training sessions too. Your Ruth Maguire is already on the Ulster team,' Lee said, spotting Ruth whizzing past.

Back in the locker room, Coach Parker approached Ayeisha. The team was celebrating their first win of the new season.

'Ayeisha, you played brilliantly. The Ulster coach was watching and asked would you like to trial for the under-16s team?' 'That would be fantastic, only I'd have no way of getting to the training sessions. My mum isn't well, so she can't take me,' Ayeisha replied unhappily.

'You can come with me – my parents won't mind,' Ruth said, sitting on the bench next to her.

Between her school, her club and the Ulster trials, Ayeisha was soon training nearly every day of the week. Fitting in her homework and chores was challenging.

One cold day in September, Ayeisha was at her computer trying to finish off an English essay when an email came in from the Ulster under-16s coach. It named the Ulster under-16s team.

Ayeisha screamed:'They picked me! I got on the team! I'm going to be the under-16s goalkeeper for Ulster!'

Ayeisha's mum had been resting on the sofa behind, and suddenly jumped with fright.

'What was that, Ayeisha?' her mum said feebly.

'Mum, I'm going to be playing in goals for the Ulster under-16s team,' she said excitedly, cuddling up next to her.

'That is the best news ever. You have made me very proud, Ayeisha,' her mum said affectionately, resting her head on her daughter's shoulder. She had recently returned from a long spell in hospital and was not feeling well. The family knew that their mum had gone downhill since being in hospital, but she had never told them how bad she felt, or just how serious her illness was.

Shortly after hearing the news of the Ulster selection, Ayeisha's mum died from breast cancer.

Ayeisha was devastated. She had lost her best friend and biggest fan.

On the morning of the funeral, the house was full of commotion.

'You look like an apple,' Shea joked when Ayeisha walked into the kitchen for breakfast.

'If I'm an apple, then you're a cucumber,' Ayeisha snapped back at her brother.

Their mum's favourite colour was green, and it had been agreed that instead of wearing black, they would all wear green to the funeral.

Ayeisha felt uncomfortable. She didn't like wearing dresses, or tights, especially green ones.

'Will you both eat your fry? You'll need all your strength; it's going to be a long day,' their Auntie Alison advised. Auntie Alison lived across the road, but had been staying with the family recently.

Ayeisha sat in the front row of the church. Nearly all of Larne Grammar School, including the teachers, had turned out for the funeral. Looking behind, Ayeisha could see her friends. She longed to sit with them, but Auntie Alison had insisted that the family must sit together.

Ayeisha looked at the coffin in the aisle and started to cry. Her family was going to be a very different one without their mum.

The pastor spoke caringly from the altar about the McFerran children and how much each of them meant to their mum.

Tamara was praised for her determination in starting

university; Reece for his mechanical inventiveness; and Shea for his passion for gardening.

When the pastor spoke of Ayeisha, he said that her mum took great pride in hearing how she had been picked to play for Ulster, and that one of her happiest memories was of their trip together to Offaly when Ayeisha won the All-Ireland Schools Javelin competition.

Before the coffin was closed, Ayeisha left her seat, leaned over the coffin and placed her All-Ireland javelin medal next to her mum. 'You will always be with me,' she whispered.

After the funeral, they returned home with Auntie Alison and their Uncle Eamonn. Uncle Eamonn had stopped off at KFC on the way to cheer them up. Her uncle was a hockey umpire, and Ayeisha always enjoyed chatting about hockey with him, bombarding him with questions about the role of the goalkeeper in a match. She learned a lot from him.

The next few days were a blur as Ayeisha returned to school. Known for being a very chatty and outgoing girl, Ayeisha now sat by herself, not saying a word. Her teachers tried their best to comfort her.

Mrs Farrell said to her quietly in Art class, 'Try to think of the funny times with your mum. It's what I did when my own mum passed away with cancer.'

'Wigs,' Ayeisha blurted out at Mrs Farrell. 'Wigs,' she repeated, half-smiling at her teacher.

'When my Mum was going through her treatment, she lost all her hair. She had loads of wigs about the house. We would steal them and try them on.'

Coach Emma Parker was very fond of Ayeisha, and was heartbroken for her. She often saw Ayeisha walking the school corridors between classes, looking glumly at the ground, and she heard that Ayeisha sat alone in the gymnasium during classes too.

One day, Coach Parker went to find Ayeisha in a school corridor. 'Come with me,' she said.

Without answering, Ayeisha followed her coach obediently. They went out through the main door and walked to the school hockey pitch.

'Now, put that on,' Coach Parker said, pointing at the familiar goalkeeper kit laid out on the ground.

'Yes, Coach,' Ayeisha replied.

'And if you ever need someone to talk to, or if you just want someone to take shots on goals, I'll be here,' she said, as she handed Ayeisha her helmet.

CHAPTER 10

ULSTER CALL-UP

'Thanks, Uncle Eamonn, see you later,' Ayeisha said as she closed the car door.

'I'm not going anywhere,' her uncle, said reaching for his umbrella.

Her uncle Eamonn liked to drop his niece off at her under-16s training sessions. It gave him a good excuse to stay and watch the best young hockey players from all over Ulster.

This was the final Ulster training session before the team departed to play in the Interprovincial Hockey Tournament at Old Alexander Hockey Club in Milltown, Dublin.

The best under-16s and under-18s hockey players

from all over Ireland would be there to represent their provinces – Ulster, Leinster, Munster and Connacht.

'Keep up, Goalie,' Zoe heckled Ayeisha as she jogged past.

Zoe Wilson was the same age as Ayeisha and played in midfield for Ulster's under-16s. The two players had immediately clicked when they met at the Ulster trials. They had since become good friends.

'I'd beat you in a race any day, and with all my goalie gear on,' Ayeisha shouted.

'I'd like to see that,' Zoe laughed.

Ayeisha liked sprinting, but dreaded running the long, slow laps around the hockey pitch with the rest of the team at the beginning and end of training.

Being a goalkeeper, Ayeisha did things differently to the outfield players. Her own drills were made up of fancy-footwork exercises, balance techniques, and learning how to react when a player came into the circle or D. A hockey goalkeeper also had to be fast on her feet, which Ayeisha certainly was.

As a young girl growing up in Larne, Ayeisha loved to play 'block in, block out' with her friends. In this game, you first had to go and hide, and then try to run back to a safe zone without being caught. Ayeisha's quick speed meant that she won a lot of the games.

Ayeisha's Irish dancing skills came in useful too. She was light on her feet and could rise up on her toes with ease. This helped her in a match when she had to change directions quickly to distract an opponent.

She also had a unique springiness about her. If she dived along the ground to save a shot, Ayeisha could spring back up onto her feet in no time at all.

There were two goalkeepers on the hockey team, as well as a reserve goalie, who would travel to matches if one of the other two goalies was injured. Claire Lowry, who was older than Ayeisha, was the other Ulster under-16s goalkeeper.

'Let's go have a kick about,' Claire said to Ayeisha after the two goalkeepers had put on their leg guards and kickers.

The first time Ayeisha met Claire, she was very nervous. At only fourteen, Ayeisha did not consider herself to be nearly as good a goalkeeper as Claire. But she was overjoyed to have been given the chance to play for Ulster. She loved goalkeeping so much.

After training, the Ulster coach handed out information to the players about the Interprovincial Hockey Tournament in Dublin. The team would be travelling to Dublin by private bus, and would be staying in a hotel for the entire weekend of the competition. Ayeisha was very excited.

On the morning of their departure, Ayeisha sat on the bus next to Hannah Grieve.

'Look, Hannah, there's Katie Mullan, she's the Captain of the under-18s Ulster team,' Ayeisha said.

'Sure I know, the under-18s Ulster team are coming on the bus with us too,' Hannah replied.

Hannah was a sweeper on the Ulster under-16s team. Her job was to keep the ball away from the goal. During matches, Ayeisha would sometimes call out to the defenders and the sweeper for help, especially if the goal area was under attack.

Hannah was very skilful in swooping in and getting the ball away, and Ayeisha was always glad when Hannah was playing in a match. Off the pitch, they enjoyed telling jokes and playing pranks on one another.

On the bus ride to Dublin, the under-16s and under-18s teams had a singing competition. The noise on the bus was deafening. The coaches couldn't quieten the girls down, so instead they joined in with the fun, taking turns themselves to sing – which made the noise on the bus even louder.

After the 'sing off', the girls passed around sweets and crisps.

Some of the under-18s players gave the younger girls tips for their matches against the other provinces.

'Leinster are your real competition,' they told them.

'When they've got the ball, the Leinster mid-fielders and forwards will all charge together at the goal.' 'Listen to your goalkeeper, as they can see best what is happening on the pitch,' they added.

As they pulled into the hotel car park, the team manager jumped off the bus. She returned a few minutes later with a large cardboard box.

'Here are your Ulster team kits,' she said.

The tracksuit was a dull grey. There wasn't even a hint of colour to it.

'That's not very cool,' an under-18s player yelled out from the back of the bus.

'All players must wear the full team kit, or they don't play,' the manager warned.

The hockey top and skort were far nicer than the tracksuit.

The top was pure white with the Ulster crest embroidered on it.

The skort was dark red, except for a single white stripe down the side.

Ayeisha looked on enviously, as the goalkeepers were only given the grey tracksuit. Then the team manager walked down to where Ayeisha was sitting and handed her a small bag. Inside was a bright yellow goalie smock. Ayeisha removed the smock and held it out by its sleeves.

'Ayeisha, you're the number one goalie!' Hannah screamed beside her.

The bright yellow smock had a large number one on the back, with 'McFerran' printed over it. Ayeisha was elated, forgetting about the ugly grey tracksuit still folded on her lap. She was the number one under-16s Ulster goalkeeper.

Ayeisha was sharing a room with her friend, and the Captain of her school team, Ruth Maguire. The two friends sat up late into the night, talking about strategy for the matches. Before going off to sleep, Ayeisha thought of her mum. She would have liked to show her the number one goalie smock.

Early the next morning, the team travelled by bus

to 'Old Alex' for their first match, against Munster.

At the side of the pitch, Ayeisha put on her goalie gear. Pulling on the last piece of kit, the number one smock, Ayeisha felt energised. She was ready for action. The match seemed to drag on, and Ayeisha saw little action in goal. The final score was 4-0.

After lunch, they played Connacht. The Ulster under-16s forwards were a force to be reckoned with again, firing six goals past the helpless Connacht goal-keeper. Ayeisha watched from the other end of the pitch, happy with the win.

The final game of the day was against Leinster. Both teams had won all of their previous matches. The winner of this match would be the under-16s Interprovincial hockey champions.

This game was completely different to the previous ones. Leinster were fast – very fast. They attacked Ulster mercilessly every time they got the ball. The Ulster defense didn't let up though, and answered Ayeisha's calls to retreat when needed.

In the final quarter, Ruth managed to get around the Leinster goalkeeper, who had strayed too far out from her goal. The ball flew up high into the net. Ulster were in front.

As the final minutes ticked down, Ayeisha stayed on high alert, determined to let nothing past her. Seeing a Leinster forward call for the ball, Ayeisha readied herself for the attack. As the Leinster player neared, Ayeisha went up on her toes, slapping away the ball with her outstretched hand pad. The ball deflected out to Hannah, who belted it away, far up the pitch.

Seconds later, the full-time whistle blew. Ulster were the under-16s Interprovincial Champions.

Leaving the pitch afterwards, Ayeisha and Ruth were stopped by a lady in a Hockey Ireland jacket.

'Congratulations, girls. Can I have your names please?' she asked formally.

'Ayeisha McFerran and Ruth Maguire,' Ayeisha replied giddily.

CHAPTER II

MOVING ON

'**Y**ou know my daughter Jordanne already – she's good friends with your sister Tamara,' Pauline said. 'And this is Victoria, our eldest.'

'Nice to meet you all,' Ayeisha replied shyly.

'I'm Nicholas, but please call me Nick,' the man said, smiling and stretching out his large hand.

Ayeisha gently shook Nick's hand. It felt rough, but warm.

Nick worked as a crewman on the boats in Larne Harbour. He also had a large garage behind their house, where he liked to fix trucks.

Ayeisha was meeting with her new foster family for the very first time, over dinner in a restaurant in

Larne town centre. The meet-up had been arranged by her social worker.

In the nine months since her mum had died, Ayeisha had been living across the road with her aunt and uncle. It was very kind of them in the first place to allow her to stay, but recently the relationship had soured. The loss of her mum had hit Ayeisha hard, and she was finding it difficult to adjust to a life without her in it.

She was becoming more of an independent fifteen-year-old, one who didn't like following rules – a rebel, you might say. Ayeisha was staying out late at night, and her aunt suspected that she was hanging out with older teenagers who drank alcohol.

One day after hockey training, a social worker was waiting for her at her aunt and uncle's house.

'Hi, Ayeisha, my name is Joanne. I'm a social worker from Foster Care Services. Your aunt tells me that you've not been happy here lately,' she said frankly.

Ayeisha was speechless, especially after hearing the words 'foster care.' She glanced up at her aunt and uncle and saw sadness in their eyes. Ayeisha understood from that moment that leaving them was the right thing to do.

'Yes, it's been difficult on all of us,' she replied.

'Well, I've found you a lovely foster family who live out in the countryside,' Joanne announced.

Ayeisha didn't like the sound of this. Countryside meant far away from where she grew up – far from her brothers and sister, her friends, her school.

'Will I have to move school?' she asked in a worried voice.

'No, Ayeisha. Luckily, you can continue on at Larne Grammar School. There is a bus near to the foster family's house that leaves at 8am,' Joanne told her.

'What about my hockey – my club? Ulster?' Ayeisha was starting to panic.

'I have spoken with the foster parents, and I told them all about your hockey,' the social worker said reassuringly.

'So what happens now?' Ayeisha asked.

'First, you should meet with the foster family – to see if they are a good fit for you,' Joanne said. 'I'll arrange a dinner meeting at a restaurant in Larne.'

Two weeks later, Ayeisha moved in with her foster family in Magheramorne, ten minutes outside of Larne.

Standing on the doorstep of her new home, Ayeisha held tightly to two black bin bags, containing everything she ever owned or cared about.

'Welcome to your new home, please come in,' Pauline greeted Ayeisha as she opened the door wide. Ayeisha stepped inside the doorway. She stood in the hallway, not moving, the black bags still in her hands.

'Would you like to see your bedroom?' Pauline offered eagerly. Ayeisha simply nodded.

The bedroom had just been decorated. There was a new bed and duvet cover, empty wooden shelves and pink-and-purple wallpaper. Ayeisha liked her new bedroom – it was very homely, she decided.

'I'll leave you to unpack and then we can sit down and have some dinner,' Pauline said, closing the bedroom door.

'Thank you,' Ayeisha replied, grateful to Pauline for giving her some time on her own to take it all in. This was a very big day for her.

Ayeisha reached into one of the black bags. She pulled out a framed picture of her mum and placed it carefully down on the empty shelf. Sitting on her new bed, she stared at the photo and smiled. 'Mum, we are home,' she said tenderly.

At dinner, Ayeisha felt awkward. She didn't say much, listening instead to the cheerful family chatter going on around the table.

After dinner, they all went into the living room. A wood burner stood in the corner of the room. Ayeisha was relieved that she was wearing shorts and a T-shirt, as the heat was stifling.

'Ayeisha, we have one rule in this house,' Nick said in a serious tone, as his two daughters, Jordanne and Victoria, looked on confused. 'There are no rules,' he laughed loudly as he offered Ayeisha a biscuit. Ayeisha liked Nick. He was funny, and had a sweet tooth like her.

'We are a family who love their chocolates and biscuits, so help yourself to anything in the cupboards,' he added.

Sitting there munching on biscuits and sipping tea with her new foster family, Ayeisha thought about Tamara, Reece and Shea. She wondered what they were doing.

Their mum had wanted her four children to stay together after she died – unfortunately, this was not possible.

At nearly eighteen, Tamara was considered an adult,

and so was left alone in the family home to take care of herself. Ayeisha knew that Tamara was well capable of this. She would be off to university in the autumn, and was more than likely busy studying for her exams.

Reece and Shea had been fortunate enough to have found a nice foster family that took them both in. Their house was at the other side of Larne to where Ayeisha was living. It had a games room with a pool table and a table tennis table. The brothers had promised to have Ayeisha over once they settled in.

'You'll have to explain the rules of hockey to me, Ayeisha, I'm a bit rusty,' Nick said, waving the packet of biscuits under Ayeisha's nose for a third time. 'And did I hear that you throw the javelin as well? Hopefully not when playing hockey!' he said with a hearty laugh that shook the entire room.

Ayeisha couldn't contain herself. Suddenly bursting out laughing, tears of joy started to stream down her face. She was going to like her new home.

CHAPTER 12

SCHOOL GAMES

'**M**ummy, that girl is holding a spear,' the child said, loud enough for everyone on the waiting train to hear.

The train was en route to Belfast. Ayeisha had walked the short distance from her new foster home to the station, carrying a small suitcase and her javelin. As she stood alone on the platform, people passing by kept staring at her.

It didn't strike Ayeisha that she was doing anything strange. She was on her way to meet the rest of her Northern Ireland schools team at Belfast airport.

Ayeisha had won the All-Ireland for javelin two years in a row. She was considered to be the top young javelin thrower in Ulster, and had been selected to represent Northern Ireland at the UK School Games in London. The competition was being held in a newly built stadium, which was to host the Olympic games only a couple of months later.

As she stepped onto the train, all heads turned to look at the girl with the spear. Ayeisha found an empty seat by the window, and laid the javelin down in the aisle close to her feet. She took out her mobile phone and called her foster mum.

'Hi, Pauline, I'm safely on the train,' she said.

'That's good to hear, Ayeisha,' Pauline replied. 'Let me know when you've met up with the others in the airport.' 'Will do. I've got to go,' Ayeisha replied hastily, seeing the ticket inspector coming into her carriage.

'Tickets please,' the ticket inspector called out as the train pulled away from the station.

Holding up her student card and ticket, Ayeisha smiled at the ticket inspector.

'And what's this monstrosity – is it some kind of weapon?' he asked, pointing at the javelin.

'That's only my javelin,' Ayeisha replied.

Seeing that the ticket inspector was none too pleased, Ayeisha added, 'I'm throwing for Northern Ireland tomorrow in the UK School Games in London.'

The ticket inspector took a moment to process this information.

'Well, the very best of luck to you, young lady. Do us proud,' he eventually said, grinning as he handed Ayeisha back her student card and ticket.

Belfast Airport was a hive of activity as Ayeisha passed through the sliding doors. She marched confidently through the terminal with her javelin held upright. As she went, crowds of travellers moved anxiously out of her way.

Ayeisha was to meet up with the rest of the Northern Ireland athletes outside the WH Smith bookshop.

'Where's your case, Ayeisha? Don't tell me you carried your javelin in your hand!' a startled-looking man said as she approached the bookshop. His name was Glenn and he was the schools organiser for Athletics Northern Ireland. He looked very important, dressed in a dark green suit and clutching a clipboard.

'I don't have a case. This is my school's javelin,' she replied honestly.

'Right so, you can put it in with the pole vault poles,' Glenn said, nodding towards a long, cylinder-shaped case covered in 'fragile' stickers.

Before boarding the plane, Ayeisha sent Pauline a short message to say that she was finally on her way to London.

Ayeisha's seat was in the middle of a row of three seats. Beside her sat fellow athletes Megan Downey and Robert Bill.

After the seatbelt sign was switched off, Glenn stood up to talk to the Northern Ireland team.

'Ayeisha, Megan, you will be sharing a room together. Robert, you're next door to them. Here's an itinerary and a schedule of events, which shows the times you will be competing at tomorrow. At the bottom is a list of emergency contact numbers,' Glenn told them.

'Could you give an example of an emergency?' Robert muttered cheekily as Glenn returned to his seat. Ayeisha and Megan began to shake with laughter.

'Hi, I'm Robert, high jumper,' he said, leaning forward to face the two girls beside him.

'Ayeisha, javelin thrower.'

'And I'm Megan, sprinter.'

'Do you play any other sports?' Robert asked.

'I'm also a hockey goalkeeper for Ulster,' Ayeisha replied.

'I've watched hockey matches. You must be very brave to be a goalkeeper, and very good to be playing for Ulster.' Robert was clearly impressed.

'I suppose I'm good at stopping goals,' Ayeisha answered humbly.

'Since you're a high jumper, I wonder have you any tips on how to jump high to reach shots? And Megan, maybe you could help me to run faster?' Ayeisha was beginning to enjoy the company of her new friends.

The flight to London went by quickly as the three young athletes talked all about sport and their excitement at competing in the school games. After arriving at their hotel, the trio spent the afternoon taking in the famous London sights.

The next morning all the young athletes assembled in the hotel reception, dressed in their Athletics Northern Ireland team kit.

'Everybody looks fantastic. This is a big day for you all,' Glenn said.

All the athletes participating in the games paraded out in a single line into the Olympic stadium. Northern Ireland was the last team out, behind the Welsh, English and Scottish athletes. The athletes walked around the oval running track before standing behind their region's flag on the central grass area.

'This is amazing,' Ayeisha said to herself, gazing around the enormous stadium. She still couldn't believe it – she would be throwing the javelin in the same venue as the real Olympics.

The javelin heats were on after the parade had finished. Ayeisha changed quickly and found a quiet spot under the stands to warm up. She stretched, lunged and touched her toes several times.

Before she had finished, a woman with a strong English accent said, 'I've never seen someone act so professional in their warm up, and you're so young as well!' Ayeisha turned around to find herself face-to-face with Alexandra Danson, the England and Great Britain hockey captain.

'You're Alex Danson!' she said, astounded.

'I am, and you are?' Alex asked.

'I'm Ayeisha McFerran. I'm a hockey goalkeeper from Northern Ireland,' she said.

'I didn't know there were any hockey matches on here today,' Alex said.

'There aren't. I'm throwing the javelin in the UK Schools Games,' Ayeisha replied.

'Well, good luck, Miss McFerran. Perhaps someday we'll meet again on a hockey pitch,' Alex said kindly.

Ayeisha was delighted to have met Alex Danson, and looked forward to telling her Ulster hockey teammates when she got home.

Ayeisha had never seen so many javelin throwers gathered together. Taking her place beside them, she thought how strange they must all look to the spectators scattered around the stands, like an ancient Roman army.

Ayeisha queued up to take her shot. The athletes had very little time to throw, and the sky quickly filled with javelins taking flight. As each athlete threw, they re-joined a long queue to go again. They each had three attempts to throw as far as they could.

Ayeisha made it into the final heat, one of the ten best young throwers from the UK. She finished eighth overall, throwing further than she had ever done before, and in the Olympic Stadium no less.

As she was placing her school javelin back into the pole vault case, Megan and Rob appeared on the grass by her side.

'Well done, Ayeisha, you did great,' they both said at once.

'I guess you are almost an Olympian now,' said Megan.

'An Olympian, I like the sound of that!' Ayeisha replied happily.

CHAPTER 13

STICK TOGETHER

'It'll fit,' Miss Parker said as she folded down the two back seats of her cute red Mini Cooper.

Getting an oversized hockey goalie kit bag into the back of a small car was never going to be straightforward.

With the seats now down, the teacher and student stood back with their hands on their hips to take in the challenge in front of them.

The two doors and boot of the Mini were open to their widest, and the passenger and driver's seats were also pulled forward. The goalkeeper bag leaned skyward against the back bumper – its straps trembled in the wind as if laughing at the two spectators.

'Ayeisha, let's do this. I'll get in the back and pull, and you push it into the boot,' her teacher said confidently.

'One ... two ... three ... push!' she called out, her body twisted uncomfortably in the narrow car door.

'Miss Parker, it's fully in,' Ayeisha said, closing the boot, relieved that the task was completed.

'We may need a bigger car, if we're going to do this twice a week,' her teacher replied, laughing.

Ayeisha's school PE teacher and hockey coach, Emma Parker, played for Randalstown Hockey Club.

Randalstown HC was a very respected club, and many of its hockey players played for Ulster and Ireland.

When Ayeisha got the short message from her PE teacher asking if she'd like to play for Randalstown Senior Women's team, she couldn't wait to get into school the next day to hear more.

Ayeisha had been getting better and better as a goalkeeper. And her good form on the pitch was attracting attention from others in hockey.

The invitation to play for the Senior Women's first team at Randalstown was a turning point in her young hockey life. For a club like Randalstown to ask you to play for them meant you must be good.

'Training is on Monday and Wednesday evenings, from 7pm to 9pm. It takes an hour to get there and back,' Miss Parker told her as she gathered up the cones after PE.

Ayeisha's excitement suddenly turned to disappointment.

'What's wrong?' her teacher asked.

'I don't know how I'll get there. With playing for the school, Larne Ladies and Ulster, Pauline and Nick are driving me around enough already,' Ayeisha replied, looking glum.

'If it's okay with your foster parents, I'll take you. After school training on Wednesdays, you can come back to my house for some food before we leave for Randalstown,' Miss Parker kindly offered.

Ayeisha wanted to hug her teacher, but she couldn't – after all, her school friends were standing nearby, and it might look a bit weird.

'Thank you so much, Miss Parker,' Ayeisha said gratefully. 'Let me help you pick up the rest of the cones.' Alice Kirby, Ayeisha's coach at Larne Ladies Hockey Club, was not surprised to hear that Ayeisha was leaving them to go to a new club.

'You have a great gift. No doubt Randalstown see

the same thing that I saw the moment I met you,' Coach Kirby said to Ayeisha at her final training session with Larne Ladies.

'You'll be missed, but you will always be welcome here at Larne Ladies,' she said sadly as the coach and ex-Larne goalkeeper walked off the pitch together.

Travelling to Randalstown with her teacher, Ayeisha was feeling nervous. She had been very much at home, on and off the pitch, at Larne Ladies. She had got to know everyone at the club – the players, their families, the umpires and even the groundskeepers.

As a hockey goalkeeper, part of your job is to communicate with your team. This is especially important when calling out warnings to your defenders during a match. The thought of having to shout instructions at players at a new club, players who were older and more experienced, made her feel very awkward.

Ayeisha was also quite shy, particularly when it came to meeting new people for the first time. Luckily, meeting her new Randalstown team couldn't have gone any better. They were all really friendly, and delighted that Ayeisha would be taking over as the number one goalkeeper for the senior team.

'Try it on,' they said, crowding around the Mini as Ayeisha struggled to remove her kitbag, wedged into the tiny boot.

The goalie smock still had the previous goalie's name printed over the number '1' – 'Teggarty'. Ayeisha was very impressed by this, as Emma Teggarty was considered one of the best goalkeepers in all of Ireland.

'At least help her with the bag,' Miss Parker shouted at her teammates playfully.

'Hi, Ayeisha, I'm CJ. Are you looking forward to playing against Hermes Hockey Club this evening?' a girl with long brown hair asked, grabbing hold of the kit bag and freeing it from the boot. She was the same age as Ayeisha and was wearing the team kit – a grey and green jersey and skort.

'A match, today? I thought it was only training!' Ayeisha exclaimed.

'You weren't saying much in the car ride up,' said her PE teacher Emma, 'so I didn't want to make you more nervous. And besides, I'll be in front of you playing in defence.' It was an altogether different type of match than Ayeisha was used to – the speed of the game, the skill of the players on both teams, and of course the number of shots on target, were all higher than she had ever experienced.

It was no wonder then that Ayeisha recognised some of the names on the backs of the jerseys – plenty of these girls were Irish Senior International players.

'Miss Parker, watch number twelve. Miss Parker, number twelve!' Ayeisha called frantically as Lisa Jacobs of Hermes HC – and Ireland – whacked the ball, which magically flew between the small gap between Ayeisha's elbow and her hand pad, landing in the goal behind her.

'I think it's probably best you call me just Parker,' her PE teacher said, scooping the ball out of the goal with her stick.

Katherine Elkin of Randalstown – and a forward player for the Irish team – levelled the score just before the final whistle.

Getting the goalie kit bag into the Mini proved easier the second time around. Ayeisha was in great form. She had just played her first match at her new club, and against Senior International players no less.

'Well, what do you think of your new club?' her teacher asked the new Randalstown goalkeeper.

'It's fantastic, Parker!' Ayeisha said mischievously.

CHAPTER 14

YOUNG IRELAND

'Ayeisha, did you see the list on the Hockey Ireland website?' Ruth asked excitedly.

'What list?' Ayeisha replied, struggling to hear Ruth over the loud banging coming from the garage behind the house. Nick, her foster father, was out there working on an old truck. She didn't mind the noise too much, as it reminded her of her brother Reece.

'The under-16s Irish team – we got on, no more trials!' Ruth shouted down the phone.

Since the Interprovincial Hockey Tournament, Ayeisha and Ruth had been attending trials for Ireland's under-16s team.

Over the past few months, the friends had travelled down to Dublin with Ruth's mum each weekend for the trials. Ruth's family had been very kind to Ayeisha – not only giving her a lift, but also putting her up in the Radisson Blu hotel with them. The hotel was near to UCD, where the trials were taking place. Ayeisha was very grateful to the Maguire family.

They played game after game on the hockey pitch at UCD as the Irish coaches moved about, sizing up all the players.

There was little time for the players to get to know one another. This didn't matter to Ayeisha – she only cared about doing her very best and getting noticed by the Irish coaches. Six goalkeepers from around Ireland had been invited to the trials, and only two would be chosen for the final team.

A week after hearing from Ruth, a package arrived for Ayeisha.

'Ayeisha, there's a delivery for you with a Hockey Ireland stamp on it. It looks important,' Pauline called from the hall door.

Ayeisha raced out of her bedroom, nearly knocking over her foster sister, Jordanne.

'Sorry, Jordanne!' she yelled.

Ayeisha and Pauline gazed at the unopened box.

'Well, are you going to open it?' Pauline asked.

'Give it here,' Nick said, appearing at the door and reaching for the box, his hands covered in oil and grease.

'No way,' Ayeisha screamed, grabbing hold of it as Nick pushed by both of them laughing.

At the kitchen table, she slowly opened the box. On top of green fancy tissue paper was a note from an Irish team coach, Kim Daly. 'You'll need these for Spain,' it said.

Beneath the tissue was Ayeisha's first Ireland kit – an oversized yellow goalkeeper smock, green shorts and socks, and the Irish team tracksuit. A glossy brochure rested at the bottom of the box, with information on the EuroHockey Youth Champion-ship in Valencia, Spain.

'I'm going to be playing in Spain!' Ayeisha shrieked.

Pauline nearly knocked over the pot of potatoes with the fright.

'That's wonderful, Ayeisha. When we are in Bally-mena tomorrow, we can pick up some suntan lotion for that beautiful pale skin of yours,' Pauline said.

Ayeisha's first match playing for Ireland's under-16s was against one of the best hockey teams in the world, the Netherlands.

The Dutch team trooped out onto the pitch before the match dressed in orange vests and skorts, looking very serious indeed. They were all very tall!

After the national anthems had played, Zoe Wilson from Ireland stood beside the tall Dutch forward, Maxime Kersholt. Ayeisha tried hard not to laugh as Maxime bent down to shake hands with Zoe.

'They are going to come at us fast,' said Kim Daly, the Irish coach, in the team huddle. 'You'll be kept going in goals, Ayeisha,' she added as the team dispersed.

'Looking forward to it, Coach,' she replied, jogging off happily.

Placing her water bottle behind the goal, Ayeisha took a few breaths to calm herself.

The match started, and the Dutch were quickly down into the circle in front of the Irish goal, firing shots at Ayeisha.

Ayeisha could feel the power of the shots through her hand pad and leg guards as she dived, jumped and lunged to stop the ball.

Her hands and legs ached as she came off the pitch after the first quarter. The Dutch had scored three goals in only fifteen minutes. Ayeisha was glad of the two-minute rest. She was disappointed that three goals had got past her, but the match wasn't over yet and Ireland could still score.

'We can do it, Lena,' she said to Elena Tice as they stepped back onto the pitch.

'They are so quick!' Elena replied.

Ireland struggled again to keep the Dutch out of their circle in the next two quarters. Ayeisha was under fire the whole time. She found it difficult to keep track of the ball with the Dutch and Irish battling it out in front of her. Hockey sticks clattered and penalty corners were given as Irish feet accidentally met with the ball.

Going into the final quarter, Ireland was losing 5-0 when Ayeisha slipped and fell onto the ball. Hockey sticks prodded her on the ground as she tried desperately to get up. The umpire finally blew her whistle, awarding a penalty stroke to the Dutch. The Irish goalkeeper had caused a foul by trapping the ball underneath her.

Standing with her two feet on the goal line, Ayeisha watched the Dutch Captain, Krekelaar, step up to the penalty spot. She had only one chance to score, no rebounds were allowed.

Krekelaar scooped the ball to the left. Ayeisha made a dive and her hand pad clipped the ball, knocking it wide. No goal. The Dutch Captain looked on in amazement. Krekelaar was the under-16s top scorer for the Netherlands and had a flawless record in scoring penalty strokes.

The match restarted quickly and Ayeisha was once again fending off an attack from the Dutch forwards. The final whistle eventually blew. 7-0. Ayeisha was annoyed and exhausted.

She kept her helmet on as she walked very slowly towards the Irish dugout. The rest of her team were already there, sitting along the benches with towels over their heads. Nobody was saying much.

'You saved a penalty stroke, and against the Dutch!' Kim roared, running up to Ayeisha on the pitch.

Ayeisha was puzzled by her coach's excitement. Had they not just lost badly to the Netherlands?

'A penalty stroke, a penalty stroke!' she repeated, grabbing Ayeisha and shaking her by the shoulders.

'Here, you deserve this,' Kim said, thrusting a small, shiny object into Ayeisha's hand.

'What's this?' Ayeisha asked, looking at a small pin with the Hockey Ireland crest on it.

'It's your first international pin for playing for Ireland,' Kim said. 'The first of many I bet, Ayeisha.'

CHAPTER 15

CAP IT OFF!

Soon after the school Christmas holidays at Larne Grammar, a call came through to the staffroom.

'Hello, Miss Parker. My name is Darren Smith and I'm the Head Coach of the Women's Irish Senior hockey team. I was wondering if Ayeisha McFerran would be free to play in reserve for the team in Spain next week?' he asked.

Ayeisha had been attending sessions in Dublin with the Irish goalie coach Nigel Henderson, aka Nidge, and had caught the eye of the Ireland Senior Head Coach.

The goalie sessions with Nidge had been the hardest ones Ayeisha had ever done. During one practice,

111

she was struck hard on the arm by the ball. She had to keep her helmet on so that the other players wouldn't see the tears running down her face.

'She's in class at the moment, Darren, but let me speak with her and ring you back,' Emma Parker replied.

Miss Parker called for Ayeisha over the school intercom. Ayeisha was sitting in Art class at the time. Her classmates jeered as Ayeisha stood up to leave, thinking she must be in trouble.

Ayeisha had great respect for her PE teacher and school hockey coach. After her mum died, Miss Parker had been very caring towards her, always providing a kind ear or a shoulder to cry on. 'Parker' was also Ayeisha's favourite defender at their club, Randalstown.

'You might want to sit down. I had an important call earlier,' Miss Parker said in a serious tone, as Ayeisha slowly entered the office.

'From who? From who?' Ayeisha pleaded, becoming slightly anxious as she squirmed in her seat.

'The Irish Senior Women's Head Coach is looking for you to play in reserve in Spain next week!' Miss Parker screamed out in delight.

Ayeisha was both surprised and thrilled, and couldn't wait to tell her friends. When she got back to class, her friends pounced on her to find out the gossip. 'Did you get in trouble? What happened?'

'I'm going to be in Spain for my eighteenth birthday with the Irish Senior team,' Ayeisha said happily, as she struggled by them and into her desk.

'Do you think you'll get to play?' Kerry asked excitedly.

'I don't know, I'm the reserve goalkeeper, but it would be great if I did,' Ayeisha said dreamily. Ayeisha had trained with some of the Senior players, but had never played in a real match with them.

Meeting the Seniors all together as a team in the airport was daunting. They were her heroes – Ayeisha couldn't believe she was actually on her way to another country with them.

The Irish team were travelling to play matches against the local side in Terrassa, in the Catalonia region of Spain. Although Ayeisha had been to Spain before with the under-16s Irish team, an eighteenth birthday and a chance to play with Ireland's super Senior hockey team was bound to be unforgettable.

Ayeisha was awoken the next morning by the bright, hot Spanish sun. She dressed quickly to arrive early for the 8am team talk. When she opened the door to the meeting room, a cry of 'Happy Birthday!' rang out from the entire Irish team and coaching staff.

'These are from your foster mum Pauline. She had arranged to meet with me in the airport car park before we left – we had to keep it a secret from you,' Zoe Wilson said, swinging a bag jammed full of presents. Ayeisha was speechless.

'Happy eighteenth, Ayeisha. This is for you too,' Emma Gray said, unfolding an Irish Senior team goalie smock, her face disappearing behind it.

Emma Gray was the team's number one goalkeeper. Ayeisha had got to know Emma at Nidge's goalie sessions. She was a fantastic keeper who Ayeisha admired.

'And congratulations on getting your first Senior cap for Ireland,' Emma announced, presenting Ayeisha with a dark green cap with gold stitching around its edges.

'No celebrating tonight – maybe just a slice of birthday cake after dinner. We want you fighting fit for your Irish debut in tomorrow's game. You'll be going on for the final two quarters,' the Irish Assistant Coach, Graham Shaw, said.

Ayeisha was overcome. She hadn't eaten breakfast yet and in her hands was her first Irish cap.

On the day of the match, Ayeisha warmed up alongside the Irish team. She listened carefully to advice from Emma Gray and watched her closely throughout the first half.

When it was time for her to go on, the score was 2-0 to Ireland.

'Use your voice, Ayeisha, you must talk to us,' Shirley McCay shouted after a Spanish shot hit off an Irish player and went into the Irish goal.

The pace was much faster than Ayeisha was used to, and she struggled to read the game. The next two Spanish goals that went in were scrappy ones, and Ireland failed to score down the other end of the pitch in the third and fourth quarter.

At the full-time whistle, Ayeisha had mixed emotions. It was her first international game and her first cap for Ireland, but three goals had found their way past her.

In the full-time team huddle, Ayeisha was silent.

'Girls, we were terrible in the second half of the match,' McCay said angrily. 'We gave our keeper no help. Sorry, Ayeisha,'

Before leaving for home, Graham Shaw spoke to Ayeisha on her own.

'You have a big future in this Irish team, Ayeisha. Keep training hard and we'll see you again very soon,' he said.

Ayeisha immediately felt better. Her Irish international journey had only started – her best performances were yet to come.

In school assembly after Ayeisha returned from Spain, her teachers praised her achievements in front of the whole school.

Miss Parker never stopped smiling throughout.

A local newspaper took photos of Ayeisha holding her Irish jersey. They published a glowing article about the Larne girl – Ireland's youngest ever hockey goalkeeper.

CHAPTER 16

SPREADING HER WINGS

Ayeisha's big plan for when she finished school at Larne Grammar was to go to college in Dublin. When the Irish team was travelling, some of the players would talk about how much they enjoyed college life in Dublin, especially playing hockey there.

'You'd love it, Ayeisha,' Anna and Chloe said one morning while waiting for their team bus.

'I've never lived anywhere else, but it really does sound exciting,' Ayeisha said.

At the end-of-season club dinner, Ayeisha told her Randalstown teammates and coaches about her big plans. It meant she would be leaving the club.

Everybody was upset, especially Ayeisha. She had played three seasons at Randalstown and had wonderful memories playing for the club. She had also made great friends. She would always be grateful to Randalstown for making her the player that she is today.

'Thanks again for everything, Parker, I really enjoyed our little chats in the Mini,' Ayeisha said to her Larne Grammar PE teacher.

'You'll have to go back to calling me Miss Parker now that you're leaving us,' Emma said, hugging Ayeisha.

'Maybe now we'll get a chance to play against you. You might go easy on us,' Zoe said, joining in on the hug.

'Of course not. You know the rules – if you're not in the same colour jersey as me, then you're against me,' Ayeisha chuckled.

During the summer break, Ayeisha received a letter from University College Dublin, saying she had been awarded a sports scholarship. The scholarship would pay for her course, but not the whole cost of her accommodation.

Ayeisha tried to find a place to live in Dublin, but everywhere was really expensive, even places very far from the college. And besides, she didn't like the idea of pulling her goalie bag across a place the size of Dublin for training and matches.

Ayeisha decided to stay in Northern Ireland. She would work several jobs to save up to go to college the following year.

'Did I hear that you're not playing for a club?' the voice at the other end of the phone said.

'Yes, who is this?' Ayeisha asked.

'It's Arlene. Would you like to come and play for me at Pegasus?'

Pegasus was one of the best hockey clubs in Ireland and Arlene Boyles was a coach there. Ayeisha had first met Arlene when she was training with the Irish Women's Senior team. Arlene was on the coaching panel with Darren Smith.

'Absolutely, Arlene, when can I start?' Ayeisha speedily replied.

'Training's this evening, if you can make it down?' Arlene asked.

'I'll be there, Coach,' Ayeisha said eagerly.

Ayeisha had played against Pegasus with Randalstown and knew well what they were capable of. Teams that played against them found them to be quite stand-offish, so she was a little nervous that she might not fit in at the club.

Ayeisha arrived early at Pegasus Hockey Club. She

always felt it was important to show her commitment by being punctual.

'Fancy seeing you here, goalie,' a familiar voice said teasingly. Ayeisha turned around to see Ruth Maguire and Hannah Grieve in Pegasus red tops.

She felt better seeing her friends. And as the rest of the team arrived and more friendly faces appeared, Ayeisha soon forgot to worry about fitting in.

After her first training session with Pegasus, Ayeisha understood why the club did so well in competitions. She was very impressed by the quality and experience of the players on her new team, and with Arlene's support on the bench, the team would always strive to do their best.

Ayeisha's first major competition playing in goals for Pegasus was in the semi-final of the Women's Irish Hockey League at Three Rock Rovers in Dublin. Pegasus was to play UCD in the semi-final. Ayeisha's Irish teammates Katie Mullan and Chloe Watkins would be playing for UCD.

As their Irish goalkeeper, Ayeisha liked to think she knew how the girls played. She had saved their shots at training, and had watched from the other end of the pitch as they scored against difficult opponents.

Katie and Chloe were not just good, but excellent hockey players.

Throughout the semi-final clash with UCD at Three Rock Rovers, Ayeisha was kept going between the posts. Hannah Grieve, in defense for Pegasus, never strayed too far from her side.

In the third quarter, Ayeisha was tracking the blonde ponytail of Chloe Watkins outside of the circle, when Chloe received a fast pass from Katie at midfield. Chloe charged and shot the ball in a way that Ayeisha had never seen any player do before.

Chloe dragged the ball across the ground and then flicked it up quickly. It travelled through the air, the ball deciding on its own where it would go. Ayeisha didn't know what to do. Luckily, her stick was fully extended and the ball hit the hook. Ayeisha was gobsmacked. Still facing Chloe, she mouthed: AMAZING!

Ayeisha did eventually surrender to a late shot on target by Katie Mullan, but Pegasus won the semi-final 2-1.

Pegasus's opponents in the final, Loreto, included more of Ayeisha's Irish teammates, such as Nicci Daly, Ali Meeke, Hayley Mulcahy and Hannah Mathews.

Ayeisha desperately wanted her team, Pegasus, to win. If they did, then she could brag about the victory at the next Irish training session!

The sides were level all the way through, until the final few minutes, when Hannah Mathews was fouled and was awarded a penalty stroke for Loreto. This was crunch time for Ayeisha, as penalty strokes were not always easy on the goalkeeper.

As Hannah stepped up to the penalty spot, the two Irish teammates eyed one another. This was not the time to be friends. Hannah took the shot quickly. Ayeisha tipped the ball; it hit off the crossbar and fell lifeless onto the ground. The full-time whistle blew – shoot-outs.

'Yes, it's showtime,' Ayeisha said to Hannah, as the Loreto player gazed in disbelief at the ball sitting in front of the goal.

Ayeisha remained on the pitch, her full attention on the job ahead.

Ali Meeke was up first, to try to score within the eight seconds allowed. Ayeisha ran out fast, arms up, her body exploding. Ali couldn't get around the Pegasus goalie as she weaved about – the whistle blew at eight seconds.

The next two Loreto shooters were also talented players from the Irish squad, Nicci and Hayley. This was not your typical club match battle – this was Ireland versus Ireland, and all the skill and talent that went with it.

Ayeisha's focus won out as she prevented the two shots from getting past her. Pegasus had won the Women's Irish Hockey League on shoot-outs!

During the trophy presentation, Ayeisha spotted her losing Irish teammates from UCD and Loreto clapping from behind the dugout.

'Hey Chloe, Kate, Nicci, I cannot wait for our next Irish training session,' she shouted over.

'Ayeisha, are you going up?' Arlene called from the dugout, disturbing Ayeisha from her banter with her Irish pals.

'But isn't the team Captain supposed to collect the winner's trophy?' Ayeisha replied, looking puzzled.

'They are, but they just announced the "Goalkeeper of the Tournament",' Arlene said. 'And that is most definitely you.'

CHAPTER 17

HOT MILK

Unlike most of the girls on the Irish team, Ayeisha wasn't a fan of coffee. She found a drink of milk to be more calming, especially on a big match day.

Before the team talk in the Killiney Court Hotel on the day of the Hockey World League 2 semi-final, Ayeisha ordered a glass of hot milk from the hotel reception. She lingered around the foyer, waiting for it to arrive, but it never came.

During a key moment in the meeting, when Head Coach Darren Smith was addressing the team, there was a knock on the door.

'Hot milk – did someone order a hot milk?' a short, elderly lady called out, scanning the room for any takers.

124

Ayeisha melted like cheese into her chair, her face turning a beetroot colour.

'Me,' she said timidly with her arm raised up in the air. The girls on the Irish team all sniggered. Darren was unimpressed by the interruption, and stopped the meeting as Ayeisha was delivered her hot milk.

The milk must have done the trick though, as Ireland defeated Belarus by seven goals to nil, winning a place in the final against Canada.

The final was being played at home in Belfield. If they beat Canada, they would not only be League 2 winners, but would have a chance to play in the qualifiers for the Rio Olympics. Ayeisha made sure she was sitting up and paying full attention at the final team talk – no milk had been ordered.

As they all listened carefully to Darren, a knock came at the door.

'Hot milk – did someone order a hot milk?' the same lady said, sneaking into the room.

Ayeisha began to slide down in her seat as the lady approached her.

'But I didn't order any milk,' Ayeisha said awkwardly, feeling all eyes again upon her.

'That's for me,' Head Coach Darren called from the top of the room.

The room erupted into laughter.

'For good luck,' he said, raising the glass and winking at Ayeisha.

After the meeting, Ayeisha spoke privately to Darren about her concerns for the Canadian match.

'Are you sure you want to put me on?' she asked her Head Coach as he took a sip from his glass of lukewarm milk.

'Yes, Ayeisha, if it ends up being a draw and goes to a penalty shoot-out, then you're on,' Darren replied as he erased the match game plan off the whiteboard.

In goalie training with Nidge, Ayeisha had demonstrated how quick and agile she was at doing penalty shoot-outs. The other goalkeepers on the squad were amazed at how good she was.

But Ayeisha knew that doing shoot-out drills over and over again was completely different to doing it in a tournament.

During the Canadian match, Ayeisha paced up and down the sideline, watching closely how each of the Canadian players behaved with the ball, in case any of them came up against her in a penalty shoot-out.

With minutes to go in the final quarter, her coach sidled up next to her and said, 'Put your helmet on, it's time to get ready.'

When the full-time whistle blew, Ayeisha was already waiting by the corner of the pitch, ready to go on. As she walked over to the goal, the packed crowd in Belfield started calling out her name.

'That's weird, how do they know my name?' she wondered, looking at the sea of faces all watching her as she moved into goal.

The first Canadian penalty shooter spun around as she arrived at the kickers of the Irish keeper. Ayeisha stepped back, disappearing out of view. The player turned again, only for Ayeisha to swoop in and kick the ball away off the pitch.

The penalties came fast and furious, each team desperate to win. Ayeisha reminded herself what Nidge had said: stay up, don't dive and *don't* let the ball in.

Each penalty taker had eight seconds to attempt to score, but Ayeisha had her own rule – she would ignore the eight-second whistle and fight until the ball was either saved or sent wide.

When Ayeisha saved the final penalty, Ireland had beaten Canada and won the Hockey Women's League 2.

They would now have a chance to qualify for the Rio Olympics!

Nikki Evans was the first across the pitch to her, the rest of the Green Army following closely behind.

'You are our shoot-out queen!' she cried joyously. Ayeisha was relieved. She had done the job her coach had asked her to do.

Two months later, Ireland were playing China, in the match that would decide what team would qualify for the Olympics.

Ireland were playing very well, but the match had not been going their way. Any time the umpire made a fair call in favour of Ireland, China would complain until the umpire changed her mind.

The Irish scored a goal against the Chinese in the final minute, a goal that would have sent them to the Olympics, but the umpire disallowed it.

'If this ends up in a shoot-out, it's not fair,' Ayeisha said.

When the match eventually finished in a draw, the Irish players were angry that after playing as they did, they were facing a shoot-out.

Ayeisha readied herself for the shoot-out against China.

She expertly saved the first three penalty shots, but the Chinese goalkeeper also did the same against Ireland.

When it was Ireland's turn to take their final penalty, it hit the post.

It was all up to Ayeisha now. If she didn't save the next penalty, there would be no Olympics.

The Chinese player and Ayeisha danced with one another until Ayeisha was forced to make a dive for the ball. Being on the ground was the most dangerous place for a hockey goalkeeper to be.

Ayeisha looked up as the ball leapt over her stick.

She didn't see the ball going into the goal, or hear the eight-second whistle blow. Lying on the ground, she saw only the legs of the Chinese players running towards her, and their penalty shooter still standing over her. China had scored. China had won.

Ayeisha wanted the ground to swallow her up.

In the sky above her she saw a plane. 'I wonder where they are going? Probably some far-flung place like America,' she wondered. 'I wish I was there now.' she said out loud as Nikki stretched out her hand to help her teammate up.

CHAPTER 18

ALL AMERICAN

Ayeisha looked up at the board. 'Delayed,' it flickered.

Everything had been going so well up to now. The taxi had collected Ayeisha at 5am to take her to the bus station in Belfast. The bus had arrived at Dublin airport right on time. The flight to Chicago actually landed early, and getting through US customs was a breeze.

'Abby? It's Ayeisha. The flight to Louisville from Chicago is delayed by four hours,' Ayeisha said slowly, suspecting that Abby might not be used to her Irish accent yet.

'That's okay, we'll see you later,' Abby replied.

Abby was Ayeisha's 'Big Sister' at the University of Louisville. A Big Sister looked after new students coming to the University, especially those from abroad. Abby was also a member of Ayeisha's new field hockey team, the Louisville Cardinals.

Ayeisha had been awarded a full scholarship to study and play hockey at the University of Louisville, in the southern US state of Kentucky.

It was well after dark when the wheels of the plane touched down in Louisville. Ayeisha was exhausted. As she took her first step out of the plane, the humidity of the August night hit her like a brick wall.

An even warmer welcome was awaiting as she walked nervously into the airport arrivals hall.

A gang of girls dressed in red-and-black vests encircled her. On the front of their vests was the head of a red bird with a yellow beak, the mascot of her new university, a cardinal bird.

'You made it,' said a blonde girl with a smile that stretched from ear to ear. 'I'm Abby, welcome to Louisville.'

Ayeisha was overwhelmed. Everyone was so nice.

The University of Louisville was only a short drive away. Ayeisha would share an apartment on campus with another first-year student. Her name was Taylor and she was a midfield player on the team.

'Help yourself to anything of mine – food, bed-clothes, whatever you need,' Taylor said generously.

'Thanks a mil,' Ayeisha replied.

'Your accent is so cool!' Taylor said in wonderment.

Ayeisha and Taylor lived across from two other hockey players, Maria and Annie.

Ayeisha fell straight into her new bed late that night, still dressed in the clothes she left Belfast in.

The aroma of freshly cut grass wafted through the bedroom window of Ayeisha's apartment. It was the perfect way to wake up after a very long trip.

The first thing Ayeisha noticed as she strolled around her new university was how vast the sports facilities were. Everything was on such a large scale. Ayeisha had never seen anything like it before.

'This is unbelievable,' she said to her guide and Big Sister, Abby.

'Wait until you see what's beside the hockey pitch,' Abby replied.

'I know that smell,' Ayeisha said as they entered the hockey grounds.

'It can put you right off your training,' Abby replied as she pointed towards the golden arches of a McDonalds restaurant, only feet away from the pitch. Both girls laughed.

As well as going to class, Ayeisha would train and play matches for the university, six days a week.

The goalkeeper was treated the same way as an outfield player, which Ayeisha was not used to. This included plenty of long runs, which Ayeisha wasn't a fan of!

The Head Coach of the Cardinals was Justine Sowry, a former goalkeeper from Australia. Justine was one of the reasons Ayeisha had been drawn to Louisville in the first place.

On a match weekend, the hockey stadium came alive.

The US anthem played before the match, the stands were full of spectators, the college band marched, and an announcer introduced each of the players as their images appeared on big screens around the stadium. Ayeisha thought it very American, but in a good way.

During Ayeisha's four years playing in Louisville, she won the All-American Award, an award only given to very outstanding athletes. She was the only student athlete in the history of the university to win it four times.

'You're getting your own banner!' Maria screamed through the door of the apartment.

Ayeisha pressed her face into her pillow. A banner meant photographers, her picture enlarged, and the big unveiling after an important match in front of spectators.

Ayeisha was proud of her achievements, but didn't like the spotlight being focused on her. Hockey is a team sport, she would argue, and the goalkeeper is part of the team, and shouldn't be treated any differently.

On the day of the big reveal, Ayeisha stood awkwardly next to the covered banner as the crowd chanted 'Three … two …one …' It helped her nerves though that they had won their match earlier!

The cover was pulled away and Ayeisha saw herself as a giant in red and black, kitted out in full goalie gear, with the years of her All-American Awards displayed underneath.

Cameras flashed and her Cardinals teammates cheered, as Head Coach Justine said nice things about Ayeisha that made her blush.

Throughout her time at the University of Louisville, Ayeisha won many awards. If you walk the corridors of the university, you will see Ayeisha McFerran listed as having made a record number of saves, and her name on numerous trophies and plaques, as well as a huge, slightly menacing poster of her hanging in the coaching office.

Attend a Cardinals hockey match at their home ground and you can't miss the giant-sized banner of the Irish goalkeeper who has won an All-American Award four times in a row.

Ayeisha was most humbled though by winning the Player's Player Award, voted on by her very own Cardinals teammates.

In Ayeisha's final year, she had a meeting with her head coach. She was due to fly to London, to play for Ireland in the Women's World Hockey Cup.

'When can we expect you back?' Justine asked, sorry to be losing her best goalie during the season.

'I'm not sure, Coach. It's the World Cup, and Ireland are ranked second from the bottom.'

'That may be so, but no other team has you, Ayeisha,' Justine said.

CHAPTER 19

THE UNDERDOGS

'We are being called the tournament underdogs. I like the sound of that,' Chloe said, peering up boldly from her newspaper.

The Ireland team had arrived into their hotel in Canary Wharf, in the business district of London, for the 2018 Hockey World Cup. The Irish goalkeeper and midfielder were sharing a room.

'That means no one knows what we are capable of,' Ayeisha replied, grinning devilishly back at her.

'I cannot wait until we prove them all wrong,' Chloe said, hurling the crumpled newspaper at Ayeisha, who swatted it away with ease.

Sixteen of the best national hockey teams from around the world were competing in the tournament, and it seemed that they were all staying in the same hotel as the Irish team!

'This is chaotic,' Ayeisha said, joining the queue, as hockey players from every country competed to find a seat to have breakfast at.

'We'd better not be late for the team talk or we'll have to sing,' Chloe said nervously.

'I'm never late, so let's eat and run,' Ayeisha replied.

The Irish team had a rule about team meetings – if you were late, you had to sing in public as a punishment! Ayeisha had never been late for a meeting.

She couldn't say the same for some of her team-mates, like Megan Frazer, but then again, Megan did have a nice singing voice! Even their Head Coach, Graham Shaw, had been caught out several times.

Ireland's first match in their group was against the USA.

'This is huge,' Anna said, coming out of the tunnel and onto the pitch of the Lee Valley Hockey and Tennis Centre. The newly built viewing stands leaned upwards into the sky. The players' families and friends were barely visible, green dots scattered around the stadium.

Ireland was quick off the mark in the first quarter of the match, with goals coming from both Deirdre

'Dibs' Duke and Shirley McCay. Dibs received a fantastic long ball from the Ireland defense, and ran around the USA goalie, tapping the ball over the line to score. McCay made a terrific sweep right on the edge of the circle, sending the ball under the keeper and into the back of the net.

The USA narrowed the gap by one goal with a player deflection that Ayeisha was powerless to do anything about.

In the second quarter, the ball hit the Irish crossbar and landed at a USA stick. Ayeisha dived, and the shot rebounded away safely.

The third quarter saw another goal by Dibs, with a shot right on target taken at the penalty spot.

In the final quarter, Ayeisha did something she had not done before as a goalie – she made a dive down on her left side to block a shot. When the stadium horn blew, Ireland had won 3-1.

'Where did that last save come from?' Nidge asked as Ayeisha pulled off her helmet, revealing a grinning goalie.

'It just came naturally, but I won't forget it in a hurry,' Ayeisha replied, her voice echoing as they went into the tunnel.

India was next to play Ireland, on an extremely hot afternoon in London. Ayeisha was struggling badly with the heat.

When Ireland were awarded a short corner at the Indian end, Ayeisha went behind her goal for water and to stand in the shade for a moment. This was only Ireland's second match of the tournament, but Ayeisha was beginning to notice more and more supporters in green filling up the stands.

Shirley took the short corner speedily, with a pass that bounced off Anna's stick and into the Indian goal. Cheers went up from the crowd. 1-0.

In the second quarter, Ayeisha's feet left the ground to tip a shot over the crossbar.

Minutes later, Hannah's quick thinking on the back post prevented India from levelling the scoreboard.

Before the full-time horn blew, Ayeisha put into practice a new lunge technique that she'd been working on over spring, making a key save that gave Ireland their second win in a row.

'That was tiring, and I have a terrible headache,' Ayeisha said, swamped in a wet towel.

'I'd say you have minor heatstroke,' said Arlene, the team manager, sitting down next to her in the dressing room. 'I'll mention it to Graham, and say that you are to go lightly in training tomorrow before we play England.'

Ayeisha stayed out of the sun, drank plenty of water and made it through the training session. She was feeling much better going into their third match.

An England-versus-Ireland match was bound to attract a large home crowd. When the Irish team ducked out of the tunnel, they were met with a wall of red and white. The English supporters had turned out in force.

It was never going to be an easy match, and Ayeisha was hardly afforded any rest from the attacking English forwards.

The England captain, Alex Danson, attempted a reverse shot on the Irish keeper, but Ayeisha kicked it away fiercely to midfield.

'Nice to see you again,' Ayeisha said, grinning.

Ayeisha had met the famed English hockey captain in the Olympic Stadium when she was throwing the javelin for Northern Ireland at the UK School Games.

There was no let-up from England. Two Irish defenders were passing the ball across the goal face when an English forward sprang, stealing the ball.

Ayeisha was on guard, sliding fast into the ball and returning it to the stunned Irish defenders.

In the final quarter, Ayeisha was diving and stopping shots every few seconds, determined to let nothing past her, when the ball suddenly clipped Hannah's stick and landed in the Irish net. An own goal, and 1-0 to England.

'That could have been a different score altogether,' Nidge said as he greeted Ayeisha coming off the pitch.

'I was certainly kept busy, but I was happy with how I played,' she replied.

'You should be. And guess what? We are into the quarter-finals, playing India again,' Nidge said excitedly.

The tournament underdogs, who nobody had paid any attention to, were now beginning to attract interest from the media, from other teams and from Irish fans unfamiliar with the sport of hockey.

Something big was on the horizon. Everyone sensed it.

CHAPTER 20

WORLD CLASS

'**W**ould you like a square of chocolate for luck?' Nidge asked.

'I had plenty last night, thanks,' Ayeisha chuckled.

The night before playing their first match in the tournament, against the USA, Ayeisha had sat up with Chloe munching Maltesers.

After beating the USA, it became a 'good luck' thing to do – to eat chocolate the night before a match.

Ireland's quarter-final match against India had just ended 0-0, and Ayeisha was getting ready for the shoot-out.

Ayeisha was concentrating hard on her notebook. This contained her notes on the players from the other team – who would shoot from far out; who would run in close, try a reverse shot or wait until the final few seconds to try to score.

Five players from each team take part in a shoot-out. Out of five shots, whoever scores the most wins.

'Rani's a runner, she's going to come straight at me,' Ayeisha reminded herself, looking at the Indian player preparing to shoot.

The whistle blew to start the eight seconds, and Ayeisha came out fast to meet her. Diving forward, she scooped the ball away with her hand pad.

The second penalty taker took too long to shoot, and the whistle blew before she had time to even strike the ball.

Ayeisha made it three out of three saves when she slid feet-first, forcing the ball out of reach of the third shooter.

On the fourth penalty, the Indian player hurriedly reversed into Ayeisha, and flicked the ball over the Irish goalie's stick – India had managed to score one penalty out of four.

Ireland had won two of their four penalties, after Róisín and Ali both found the back of the Indian net.

If Chloe scored the next penalty for Ireland, the gap would be too wide for India. Even if they scored their fifth penalty, Ireland would still win.

Ayeisha watched on nervously, close to the side of the pitch. She knew her roommate could do it.

It was edge-of-your-seat action as Chloe moved from side to side, taunting the Indian goalie. At the very last second, she struck the ball, launching it over the keeper and into the goal. The ball dropped behind the line just as the eight-second whistle blew. Chloe didn't disappoint, and Ireland were in the semi-finals – what an achievement!

'Help, I'm stuck in your leg guard,' Katie cried out as the Irish team leaped in celebration onto Ayeisha.

Ayeisha was breathless from the shoot-out, the heat, the gear weighing her down, and her Irish teammates now piling on top of her. If not for the loud cheers keeping her up, she would have crumpled to the ground.

'Plenty of space now,' Anna said the next morning as she carried her breakfast tray to her seat. Many of the teams competing in the tournament had left, so it was much quieter in the hotel.

Ireland was gearing up to play Spain in the semi-finals.

The team were familiar with the Spanish side, having played them several times before. They saw Spain as quite similar to themselves, and counted many of the Spanish players as friends.

As Ireland stood for the anthems, they stared in disbelief at the stands, now bulging with green supporters. It was a remarkable sight.

Early into the match, Anna 'nutmegged' the Spanish goalie from a short corner pass, striking the ball right between the unsuspecting goalie's legs.

The score stayed in Ireland's favour until after half time, when the Spanish forward, Magaz, outfoxed Ayeisha with a shot from the penalty spot that Ayeisha dived for too late. 1-1.

In the last ten seconds of the match, the crowd started counting down the clock. When the horn blew, the spectators were up on their feet screaming. It was a draw, but what was coming next was what they really wanted to see – another shoot-out.

'Show them what you can do; this is what you're good at,' Ayeisha told herself as she hit the crossbar with her stick. It was go time.

Ayeisha knew Garcia of Spain – the defender featured frequently in her notebook. Ayeisha walked out slowly; Garcia attempted a dummy shot, but the keeper's leg guards were glued together, and the ball rebounded away.

Perez showed plenty of her back to Ayeisha as she reversed into her – a splendid Irish dive robbed the Spaniard from scoring.

Ayeisha noted the number '23' stitched on the side of the next red skort – it was Oliva, the Spanish midfielder. She charged at Ayeisha like a mighty bull, flipped the ball over her left foot, and it went into the goal. Spain had their first penalty goal.

The fourth Spanish penalty was a messy one with numerous attempts, but none finding the goal.

Lola Riera claimed the fifth penalty for Spain, lobbing the ball over Ayeisha's outstretched stick.

Meanwhile, Ireland's Gill Pinder and Chloe Watkins' shots on the Spanish goalie levelled the penalty score to 2 out of 5 each.

It was sudden death – whoever missed next lost the match.

Gill revisited the top of the circle again to take her shot. Her perfect drag flick nutmegged the goalie and sent the crowd into a frenzy.

It was down to Ayeisha now. If she saved the next

penalty, they would have done the unthinkable –
Ireland, the tournament underdogs, would be playing in the final of the Hockey World Cup, for the
first time ever.

Silence fell around the stadium as Ayeisha marched
into the goal.

Behind Oliva, who was charged again with taking
the shot for Spain, the Irish team linked arms.

'Watch her stick, watch her stick,' Ayeisha whispered.

The whistle blew to start the eight seconds, and
Ayeisha crept cautiously out of the goal. Her eyes
were fixed on Oliva's stick, scraping the ground as it
moved in closer and closer.

As she reached Ayeisha, the Spaniard raised the
ball with the end of her stick to chip it past the
Irish keeper, but Ayeisha was ready for it, making
a spectacular save and clearing the ball away. It had
gone too far to try again, and the eight-second
whistle declared that Ireland were the winners.

Finding a reserve of energy from somewhere,
Ayeisha raced off the pitch and jumped on Nidge.

'We did it! We're in the final, can you believe it?' she
screamed into his ear. 'Thank you Nidge,' she added,
still holding on tightly to her Irish goalie coach.

'Now we just need Australia to beat the favourites, the Netherlands, later,' Nidge replied, embracing his queen of shoot-outs.

Back at the hotel that evening, the Irish team watched a tense match between Australia and the Netherlands. It also ended in a penalty shoot-out, and the Netherlands eventually won out. It would be Ireland versus the Netherlands in the Hockey World Cup final.

The Irish team were still giddy over their win against Spain, a win that they were beginning to treat as their own final.

Ireland, like so many hockey teams, saw the Netherlands as the best team in the world. This team played hockey full-time; they had big sponsors, and plenty of money behind them. They were the favourites to win the tournament before it had even started.

Ireland were the underdogs, but the underdogs had turned the sport upside-down, and had packed the stands with new followers of the sport.

On final day, the stadium erupted when Ireland took to the pitch. It was insane.

As the Dutch players shook hands with the Irish players before the match, they said they'd never played in an atmosphere like it.

Though Ayeisha played with all her heart, the final score was 6-0 to the Netherlands.

After the match, the Irish team jogged united around the pitch, clapping their families, friends and supporters. Among the crowd, Ayeisha saw her sister Tamara, her Louisville Cardinals Head Coach Justine, and also girls that had played with her at Randalstown. She was thrilled to see them all.

As Ireland lined up in the tunnel for the medal presentation, the Irish team manager, Arlene Boyles, yanked Ayeisha out from the line.

'You won Goalkeeper of the Tournament,' she said, excitedly pushing Ayeisha to the mouth of the tunnel.

'Are you sure, Arlene? Maybe they've made a mistake,' Ayeisha was shocked.

'No, it's you all right. Well done, Ayeisha, we are so proud of you!' Arlene said.

'But I'm still in my kickers and leg guards,' she called out as Arlene disappeared back down the tunnel to the Irish team.

'The Hockey World Cup Goalkeeper of the Tournament: Ayeisha McFerran, Ireland,' the announcer roared out through the stadium speakers.

AYEISHA McFERRAN

'Don't trip, don't trip,' Ayeisha told herself, as she stepped out of the tunnel to deafening cheers.

CHAPTER 21

WELCOME HOME

'**C**an you tell us how you felt after winning Goalkeeper of the Tournament?' the reporter asked, pointing the microphone to Ayeisha.

'Very proud – not just for me, but for the whole team,' Ayeisha replied humbly.

The Irish Women's Senior Hockey team were up early, the day after the final of the Hockey World Cup.

There was a festival atmosphere in the hotel lobby. The Irish hockey stars were pulled in different directions to answer questions, sign autographs and pose for photos.

'Ayeisha, I just heard we're flying back to Dublin on a private plane,' Lizzie said excitedly, barging in front of the news reporter.

'A private plane? I like the sound of that, Lizzie. I might even catch up on some sleep,' Ayeisha replied.

Ayeisha had only slept for a few hours the night before, as the Irish team and their families partied late into the London night. She had such a great time, and was delighted to have also met up with Justine, her coach from Louisville.

Sleep, however, was the last thing on the team's mind when their private plane took off for Dublin. Everyone started singing the team's new song, 'All I want for Christmas'.

'I should never have mentioned it,' Zoe said, wearily leaning into Ayeisha, as the song started up for the third time.

It had all begun at a training session in London. The team had been stretching in an outdoor park surrounded by tall skyscrapers, when Zoe looked up and said, 'This feels like Christmas.' From then on, before each match in the World Cup, the entire Irish team would sing 'All I want for Christmas'.

Dublin Airport was packed with supporters who had come out to welcome the Irish team home. Ayeisha even spotted her Larne Grammar Maths teacher, Mr Lambe, waving out among the horde of well-wishers. She was overjoyed too to have finally met with her Irish goalkeeping coach's wife, Kathryn.

'Nigel never stops saying what a great goalkeeper you are, Ayeisha,' Kathryn said kindly.

'That's only because I have the best goalie coach,' Ayeisha replied affectionately.

A private bus had been organised to take the team, the coaching staff and their families into Dublin City for a homecoming ceremony. A long line of police motorcycles escorted the bus on its journey into the capital.

'I feel like a pop star,' Ayeisha said, sitting next to Róisín.

'Look at everyone along the road cheering us, Ayeisha. It's mad!' Róisín replied in amazement.

When the Irish team walked out onto the stage on Dame Street, the reception they received from the thousands gathered was incredible.

Music was blasting out from giant speakers. Des Cahill, the Irish sports presenter, was speaking glowingly about the team's success in the World Cup.

'This is unbelievable,' Elena said, standing next to Ayeisha and waving out at the massive crowd.

The Irish Captain, Katie Mullan, was the first to be introduced from the team.

Katie grabbed the microphone and told the story of the talented bunch of Irish sportswomen who had stolen the hearts of the hockey world. A team like no other, who had battled hard as the tournament underdogs to get to the Hockey World Cup final. They had proved that anything is possible.

The crowd roared as each player's name was called out by the Irish Captain.

When it was the heroic Irish goalkeeper's turn to step up, she slipped shyly behind Chloe and Elena, who were standing to either side of her.

'Push her out front, girls. Let them see your Goalkeeper of the Tournament medal, Ayeisha,' Zoe heckled, stealing the microphone from Katie.

Chloe and Elena hooked Ayeisha's arms and dragged her up to Zoe and the baying Irish crowd, who were now screaming her name.

'Do you have something you want to say, Ayeisha?' Zoe asked, throwing her arm around her friend.

'Yes, I do, Zoe,' she replied as she looked back at her teammates for support, and started to sing …

'I don't want a lot for Christmas,
There is just one thing I need …'

CHAPTER 22

GOING DUTCH

'I don't know what's wrong. It's as if the pace of the games has slowed down all of a sudden. It's very frustrating,' Ayeisha said.

'It's because you were playing against the best international players in the world, and you needed to react in a different way,' her Louisville coach replied.

'What do I need to do then, Coach?' Ayeisha asked.

'A goalkeeper must learn to adapt. It'll take a few games, so don't worry too much,' Coach Sowry answered.

Ayeisha was finding it difficult to get back to normal life in Louisville after returning from the Hockey World Cup in London.

Playing under the title of Best Goalkeeper put pressure on Ayeisha to play at her very best in every match at the university. If the team lost a game, she would feel awkward, especially if she hadn't played well. But she could always count on her Cardinals teammates for their support.

The media in Louisville continued to nab her after matches to talk about the World Cup, and to praise her for shining a spotlight on goalkeeping. Coaches from opposing teams would also congratulate her on her success at the World Cup.

In her final season at the university, Ayeisha began coaching some up-and-coming young goalkeepers at the local Kentucky Hockey Academy.

On her first day at the Academy, she asked an excitable bunch of junior goalies if they had any questions before practice began. It reminded her of when she was their age, starting out at Larne Ladies Hockey Club with her coach, Alice Kirby.

'If you let in goals, does that mean you're an awful goalkeeper?' a young girl asked, drowning in an oversized goalie smock.

'Every goalie lets in goals, it's part of the job. But not every goal that goes in is your fault,' Ayeisha replied, smiling down at the bunch of youngsters. 'You have to look at each goal and ask yourself: Did you touch the ball, but it still went in? Did it hit off a player? Did your defenders help you? Did you make a mistake? Or was it just a terrific shot?'

'If it's the defenders' fault, can you give out to them?' a boy of around ten years old shouted out from the back of the group.

'Oh no, you shouldn't do that. Everybody makes mistakes. They are your teammates after all, and you want them working for you in the next match, and the match after that,' Ayeisha said kindly.

'What does the goalie do during a match if the ball is at the other end of the pitch?' the same boy asked.

'You have the best spot on the hockey pitch to see what is happening. Talk to your team and tell them what you see, and if the ball comes into the circle, make sure to talk a lot more,' she said.

'Are there any more questions before we start the practice?' the celebrated Cardinals goalkeeper asked.

'Will you autograph this?' the young girl said, swinging her helmet towards Ayeisha.

Ayeisha's graduation ceremony spelled the end of university and playing for the Louisville Cardinals. Even though it was a happy occasion, Ayeisha also felt sad, as she would be saying goodbye to close friends she had played with for over four years. Tamara, her sister, had surprised Ayeisha by flying out to be at her graduation.

It was a typical all-American graduation, with the students decked out in flat hats and black gowns. Ayeisha wore a white and red sash around her neck, which showed she was an athlete at the University.

Grand speeches were made, and each Louisville student was called up to receive their scroll from the President of the University.

'I know what I want to do after University. I want to be a full-time goalkeeper,' Ayeisha said at dinner after the ceremony.

'Are you going to stay in America?' Tamara asked.

'I'd like to play for a professional hockey team closer to home, maybe in Holland. And I know from playing against the Dutch that they all speak English there,' she replied.

Ayeisha made it known to hockey clubs throughout Europe that she was interested in playing in goals professionally.

At this time, Ireland Men's hockey goalkeeper David Harte was playing for the men's side at Kampong in Utrecht, Holland. David heard that their women's first team goalkeeper was leaving the club.

He let the coaches know that Ayeisha was available, and that they'd be wise to grab her quickly, before someone else did.

In a matter of days, Kampong were on the phone to Ayeisha's Irish goalkeeper coach, Nidge, to talk about his top player.

Ayeisha was flown out to Holland. She visited the club in Utrecht and met with the coaches. She was shown an apartment that she could live in, and her very own bike to get to training. It was perfect.

When Ayeisha met with her new Kampong teammates, she recognised many expert players from the Dutch national side. She was very impressed and knew that the standard of playing was going to be very high at Kampong.

'I remember playing against you in the under-16s Eurohockey Youth Championship in Spain. You were the Irish keeper. We still talk about the penalty stroke you saved against our Captain,' Carmen Wijsman said as she welcomed Ayeisha to the team.

Playing for Kampong was different to playing for the Cardinals. For one thing, Ayeisha didn't have to study *and* play hockey. It was non-stop hockey, and Ayeisha fitted in right away.

On Friday afternoons, Ayeisha met up with fellow Irish goalkeeper and Kampong clubmate David Harte. They were both training with the well-known Dutch goalkeeping coach Martijn Drijver.

'How are you settling in, Ayeisha? Is it different here to playing in America?' David asked, his head tipping the top crossbar.

'Well, one thing certainly stands out – there's no McDonalds at the side of the pitch,' she laughed.

CHAPTER 23

SHE'S A KEEPER

'I cannot wait to get into an ice-cold bath,' Ayeisha said during a break in the morning training session.

'Me too, it's so hot,' Anna O'Flanagan said, passing Ayeisha a bottle of water from the cooler.

Ayeisha gulped it down quickly.

'Pass me another,' she pleaded to Anna.

The Irish team were on tour in South Africa, playing friendly games against the South African host side. Ayeisha was still buzzing from hearing some great news before they left – she had been nominated as 'Best Hockey Goalkeeper in the World' by the Federation of International Hockey.

Ayeisha had very pale skin and ginger hair, so she needed to be very careful when it came to playing in hot climates. She would always drink plenty of water and wear sunscreen, and between sessions she would search out shadowy places to rest in. She would even wear an ice vest under her goalkeeping kit to keep her temperature down.

The worst thing was her helmet, which trapped all the heat rising up from her body – like a kettle boiling. When the outfield players were up at the other end of the pitch, and it was safe to do so, Ayeisha would remove her helmet and pour water over her head.

'Are you okay, Ayeisha? You look paler than usual,' Anna said worriedly.

'Not really, it must be the heat,' she replied dizzily.

Ayeisha suddenly felt her legs go weak underneath her and she stumbled into the water cooler.

Ayeisha had long been looking forward to the trip to South Africa, as it would include a very important milestone – winning her 100th cap playing for Ireland. Lying in bed back in her room, shivering and unable to eat, her 100th cap was the last thing on her mind.

'I hope you're better soon,' Anna said caringly as she packed up her suitcase to move rooms. Anna had been sharing a room with Ayeisha on the South African trip and the team coaches were now worried that Anna might get sick too.

'The thermometer is saying over forty degrees, which really is not good,' the Irish team physiotherapist, Róisín Murphy, said after checking in on Ayeisha for the fourth time.

It was 7.30pm, and Ayeisha had been in bed since ten that morning.

'You're going to the hospital,' the physio said firmly.

Ayeisha spent three days in hospital in South Africa recovering. For that whole time, she wasn't able to eat anything at all. She was attached to a hospital drip that continually fed liquids into her.

She had become quite thin, and felt very weak and poorly.

Her Irish teammates weren't allowed to visit her either, as the doctors believed she had picked up a nasty bug off the pitch itself, which might be catching.

In her training, Ayeisha had been practising her diving. When she dived, her helmet and face would sometimes come in close contact with the ground.

The pitch was sprayed with water regularly – this was to help the ball travel faster, and to stop players from tripping up on dry patches. The water may not have been the cleanest, and the incredible South African heat hammering the pitch surface might not have helped either.

Ayeisha had missed all but one match on the South African tour. Feeling slightly better, she left hospital on the morning of the last day. Ireland was to play South Africa in the afternoon.

After the team meeting, Ayeisha gazed down at the bagel with peanut butter as if it were a giant concrete block.

'If you're not going to eat it, I will,' Elena joked.

'I have to eat something, Lena, I need the energy if I want to play later,' Ayeisha replied miserably.

'Don't eat it just yet, I have something I want to give you,' Elena said.

All of a sudden, the rest of the Irish team barged into the room, cheering.

'It's your 100th cap,' Elena said, thrusting it out in front of her.

Ayeisha had completely forgotten. Her mind had been focused on trying to get better and get out of hospital to play. It was a great surprise after an awful past few days away from her teammates.

Ayeisha had played in countless matches since she started playing in goal for Ireland, but she had never felt as bad as she did in South Africa playing that afternoon. The heat and humidity were unforgiving.

Going into the second quarter, she couldn't see the ball, her helmet felt like a sauna and she started to shake all over again.

During the half-time break, Ayeisha collapsed. She was immediately rushed to the medical room, where she was once again hooked up to a drip.

Having removed her heavy goalie kit and wrapped her head in an iced towel, Ayeisha was able to walk back to the pitch. With the drip still attached to her, she sat and watched the final quarter of the game.

Sitting on the same water cooler that she had stumbled over at training, Ayeisha noticed Anna close to the sideline, leaning on her stick for support.

'Anna, are you okay? You look very pale,' she said.

'Not really Ayeisha, I feel very cold all of a sudden,' she said, shivering.

CHAPTER 24

LOCKDOWN

'I think I need a break from hockey,' Ayeisha said sorrowfully, sitting in her apartment in Utrecht, Holland.

'It's normal to feel the way you do,' Anne replied.

Anne was Ayeisha's close friend and was also a hockey goalkeeper herself.

'I've been playing hockey non-stop for the past five years, Anne, and I'm tired,' Ayeisha said bluntly.

The stress of having to constantly play at her best, to stay fit and sharp and to avoid getting injured, along with all of the travel to matches, was starting to get too much for Ayeisha.

'You won't have to worry about flying anywhere for matches if things get any worse,' Anne said as she scrolled down through the news feed on her laptop.

Countries around the world had begun announcing travel restrictions because of Covid-19 outbreaks. Lockdowns were becoming more common, sporting events were being cancelled and even club training was being restricted.

Ayeisha's own club, Kampong in Utrecht, had recently told its players that training was to be reduced to playing in small groups, or pods, of only four players. Ayeisha's break from hockey was on its way, whether she liked it or not.

With travel not possible, and no matches on the calendar, Ayeisha had some spare time to try other things.

She baked delicious banana bread for her Kampong teammates. She made hot and spicy curries and invited friends over. She did puzzles and jigsaws, went on cycling trips with Anne, and became a personal fitness trainer at her local gym.

Though Ayeisha welcomed the rest from the sport, she was afraid that if the Covid-19 situation worsened, the Olympics might be cancelled. She might not get the chance to play for Ireland in Tokyo.

'I'm very worried too,' Anne said seriously.

The Netherlands had also qualified for the Olympics, and Anne was the Dutch goalkeeper.

Their friends would often tease the goalie pair about competing against one another in the same group in the Olympics, but this didn't bother Ayeisha or Anne.

The two would share stories and give each other advice – especially when it came to playing a particular opponent. But most of all, both being goalkeepers, they each understood what this responsibility was like.

'Let's stop looking at the Internet every day,' Ayeisha said one morning over breakfast. 'We have to stop checking for updates on the Olympics.'

'You're right. We must try to be positive, and say it *is* happening. We *will* be going to Tokyo,' Anne replied confidently.

Ayeisha decided it was time to focus her attention back on her goalkeeping. The downtime from the sport had served her well, but she was keen now to get out playing matches again.

Ireland and Great Britain had arranged to play some pre-Olympic friendly matches in Belfast. Ayeisha was really excited at the thought of seeing her Irish teammates again, and also at playing against Great Britain, a team they'd never beaten before.

Arriving into Belfast from Holland, Ayeisha had to quarantine in a hotel for a week. She kept busy, having Zoom meetings with her Irish and Kampong teams. She even had gym equipment set up in her room to maintain her fitness.

As she was still in quarantine, Ayeisha missed out on the first match against Great Britain, which ended in a draw.

Players from the Irish team were placed into pods. Ayeisha's pod included Katie, Chloe and Niamh Carey. Each pod shared rooms, ate together and travelled to and from the pitch together on match days.

Niamh was a newbie to the Irish team, and the 'podders' made sure that she was included in all their chats and joking about.

No spectators were allowed at these matches, because of lockdown rules. The Irish players really missed the support of the home crowd, particularly when they had a historic win over Great Britain in their second match.

The excitement around the build-up to the Olympics was growing as official news was finally released that the Olympics in Tokyo would be going ahead.

Athletes who had qualified for the games were once again being highlighted in the press. One such athlete popped up on the radar of a major energy drink sponsor.

'Ayeisha McFerran, you will be the first female Irish athlete ever to be sponsored by us,' the Red Bull representative announced proudly.

Ayeisha was thrilled to sign a sponsorship contract with Red Bull. Best of all, she would help to design her new hockey helmet that she would wear for matches.

Red Bull would not only be promoting Ayeisha as an Irish athlete around the world – they would also be bringing awareness to hockey goalkeeping, and to women in sport, which was very important to Ayeisha.

'Don't be nervous at all. Enjoy it, you'll do great,' the Red Bull photographer said calmly.

'I'm not used to being on my own in a photo. I like having my team around me,' Ayeisha replied, perched a little uneasily on a stone step.

'You look fantastic. Here we go so,' the photographer said, preparing to shoot the new addition to the Red Bull family.

'Say "cheese". No, hang on, that's not the right word for this occasion,' he said, glancing up from his camera.

'I know – say "Olympics" …'

CHAPTER 25

GO, GREEN ARMY!

'We're hockey players, not swimmers!' Ayeisha joked, waving the goggles about in the airport queue.

'Are we landing in the sea?' Chloe asked, trying hard not to laugh along with her friend.

'They're safety goggles, in case somebody sneezes in your direction,' the Team Ireland representative said in a no-nonsense tone.

'I can't wear these for the entire flight,' Ayeisha said, starting to worry.

'You don't have to, but if any player becomes infected with Covid, there'll be no Olympics for them,' the team rep replied sternly.

Ayeisha gulped. It was her biggest dream to play

in the Olympics. She had been very careful over the previous few months, washing her hands, keeping her distance and cleaning her equipment after training. All of a sudden, the goggles didn't seem so bad.

The Irish hockey team were seated in 'business class'. It was a nice surprise as they boarded the plane in Dublin to be led by an air steward to the front of the plane, where large, comfy seats could convert into beds.

'This is the life,' Ayeisha said happily.

'It sure is,' Sarah Hawkshaw, the Irish midfielder, said, reclining comfortably in her seat.

The first stop on their Olympic journey was in Doha, the capital of Qatar, in the Middle East.

It was dark when they arrived, and the heat and humidity nearly knocked Ayeisha over as she exited the plane. Beside the plane, a bus was waiting to escort the team to a private lounge where they would rest before their final flight to Tokyo, Japan.

To keep their spirits up, and to make sure everyone was fully awake, the team sang songs by The Cranberries and stamped their feet in unison as the bus neared the airport terminal.

'Anna, this is like a five-star hotel,' Ayeisha said, strolling into the luxurious airport lounge.

'Shower, then food. Race you!' Anna replied, elbowing Ayeisha out of her way and grabbing a plush white bathrobe from a rail.

'The showers aren't going anywhere, but the food is!' Ayeisha called after her. Anna slid to a halt, turned quickly, and returned the bathrobe to the rail.

'You're right. Food it is – race you!' Anna said, darting away.

'A typical forward player, always running,' Ayeisha teased.

Full from the wonderful food that was laid on for them, Ayeisha slept comfortably for most of the plane journey from Doha to Tokyo.

At 11pm Tokyo time, the Irish hockey team touched down. Ireland was at the Olympics.

There was a carnival atmosphere in the airport's arrivals hall, as the doors slid open to reveal hordes of competing athletes from around the world dressed in their nation's colours.

'Girls, we've arrived,' their Captain, Katie Mullan, announced. Their hard work had led them to this moment; there was no going back now.

The next few hours went by in a blur. Each member of the team had several Covid-19 tests. Softly spoken

Japanese officials asked them to line up to be counted. Ayeisha's goalkeeper's bag was weighed, checked and then checked again.

Three hours after landing in Japan, the team stepped outside into the Tokyo air and straight onto a 'sleeper bus'. This would take them to Iwate, seven hours' drive to the north of Tokyo. Iwate was to be their home until the move to the athletes' Olympic Village before their first match.

'I can't seem to get comfortable. These seats are far too small,' Ayeisha cried out as she twisted in the confined space.

'They call this a sleeper bus? More like a no-sleep bus,' Zara said cheekily.

A large crowd lined the road leading up to their hotel in the early hours of the rising sun. Smiling Japanese well-wishers waved Irish flags and held banners welcoming the Irish hockey team to Iwate.

Ayeisha was glad to have her own room in the hotel. Dropping her bags inside the door, she dived face first onto her bed and didn't wake up until lunchtime.

'We will have a light training session on the pitch later, to adjust to the time difference,' Katie said at the team talk.

'I'm looking forward to seeing the pitch,' Ayeisha said to Chloe as they left the hotel.

'And to get there, we have to take a cable car up the side of a mountain,' Chloe replied gleefully.

Coming into a clearing within a lush, green forest, the Irish team spotted their hockey pitch off in the distance. At either end, log cabins had been specially built as changing rooms.

As they neared the pitch, they saw traditional Japanese dancers performing in midfield. Locals had gathered high up in the hills above the pitch, and the Mayor of Iwate was at the gate to greet the team. Beside him was a suspicious-looking row of shovels.

'I thought you said a light training session, Katie? What are the shovels for?' Ayeisha said boldly.

'Welcome to Iwate, Team Ireland,' the Mayor said, bowing.

'*Domo arigato*,' Katie replied in Japanese, nodding her head respectfully.

'In honour of your stay, we would like to plant a tree beside the hockey pitch,' the Mayor said, pointing at the shovels.

Forming a circle, the Irish team each picked up a

shovel and took it in turns to place some soil on the newly planted tree.

'Tonight we celebrate, but for now, please enjoy your new hockey pitch,' the kindly Mayor said, still grinning.

That evening, a dazzling firework display lit up the night sky over the hotel. Bright green coils shot through the air as the Irish team was treated to a marvellous feast. Favourites of the entire team were the delicious Wagyu beef and blueberry juice, both famous specialities of Iwate.

Their time in Iwate went by too fast. Ayeisha was disappointed to be leaving, but she was eager to move into the Olympic Village.

'It's not as plush as our hotel room back in Iwate, but it's really great to finally be here with the other athletes,' Ayeisha said.

'All we need is a bed and somewhere to hang our gear,' Michelle Carey, the newest member of the Irish team, replied.

Ayeisha was sharing an apartment in the Olympic Village with Michelle, Chloe, Zara, Sarah and Anna. This had been her player pod since leaving Dublin, and she liked that it gave her a chance to get to know Michelle better.

Their first Olympic match would be against South Africa. In the run-up to it, the team did outdoor yoga and played short practice matches. Ayeisha missed not having Nidge there with her, but she had promised to ring her Irish goalkeeping coach after every match.

Daily team Covid-19 testing was part of the routine in the Olympic Village. Safety was very much on everyone's mind. The team sat by themselves in the dining hall, away from other athletes.

On the eve of their first match, Ayeisha and her fellow 'podders' watched the official opening ceremony on a projector screen in their apartment.

Seeing the Irish flag carried out into the Olympic stadium, a hush fell over the room until Ayeisha broke the silence with: 'It's bedtime, girls. We've a match tomorrow.'

On 24 July 2021, the Senior Irish Women's Hockey Team awoke to play in the Olympics, the first Irish team ever to do so.

Spectators were forbidden from attending the match, but that didn't stop the Irish team from getting a wonderful reception from locals and other athletes outside of the stadium.

'This is weird,' Ayeisha said, looking around at all the empty seats as she walked out onto the pitch. She was of course glad to be at the Olympics, but she was also sad that no one could be there to see them play, particularly the Japanese people who were hosting the games.

As the Irish National Anthem played, Ayeisha glanced up and down the line at her teammates. She was proud of each and every one of them, and of herself too.

After the anthems, Ayeisha took up her position in goal. Pulling down her helmet over her face, she looked up the pitch, eagerly waiting for the whistle to blow.

'I'm an Olympian,' she said excitedly. 'So, let the games begin.'

HOCKEY TERMS

Backboard – the board that runs inside the lower part of the goal

Backline – the line along the goal post, or line which marks the width of the pitch

Back post – the far post, behind the goalkeeper

Back stick – hitting the ball with the rounded part of the stick

Circle or 'D' – the semi-circle in front of the goal

Dugout – where players sit at the side of a pitch

Foot – kicking or stopping the ball with your foot

Goalkeeper – the bravest player on the team!

Green card – given to a player who fouls and is sent off for two minutes

Kickers – worn by goalkeepers to protect their feet and ankles

Hand pads – worn by goalkeepers to stop or block

shots with their hands

Leg guards – worn by goalkeepers to protect the leg from the ankle to over the knee

Logging – when a goalkeeper makes a log shape with their body on the ground

Long corner – awarded to the other team when a defender hits the ball over the backline

Nutmeg – to score between the legs of a goal-keeper or player

Pass back – the play that begins or restarts a game, or after a goal is scored

Penalty (or short) corner – when a foul occurs within the circle

Penalty spot – where penalty shots or strokes are taken from

Penalty stroke – a shot on goal given to the other team

Pressing – getting the other team to move the ball where you want it

Push – moving the ball around by a pushing movement of the head of the stick

Quarter – field hockey games have four quarters

Referral – to question the decision of an umpire

Red card – given to a player who fouls and is sent

off for the entire match and next game

Shoot-out – a one-on-one shot against the goal-keeper of the other team

Short – short for 'penalty corner' or 'short corner'

Skort – shorts with an over-skirt

Smock – a goalkeeper's jersey

Sudden death – the first goal scored after the shoot-out ends the game

Sweeper – a defender who plays between the defensive line and the goalkeeper

Underdogs – the team that is expected to lose

Umpire – the official responsible for enforcing the rules of the game

Yellow card – given when a player fouls and is sent off for five minutes

AYEISHA McFERRAN'S
ACHIEVEMENTS

2021: Olympic Games, Toyko, Japan

2020: Redbull sponsored athlete

2019: FIH Goalkeeper of the Year – Nominee

2018: FIH Goalkeeper of the Year – Nominee

2018: World Cup – Silver Medalist

2018: FIH World Cup – Goalkeeper of the Tournament

All American 1st Team – 2016, 2017, 2018

All American 3rd Team – 2015

All ACC Tournament Team

All ACC First Team – 2016, 2017, 2018

NFHCA All-West Region First Team Selection –
  2015, 2016, 2017, 2018

2017: FIH Hockey World League Round 2 – Goalkeeper of the Tournament

2017: FIH Hockey World League Round 2 – Winners

2015: Eurohockey Championships 2 – Gold

2015: World League Round 2 – Gold

2014: Champion Challenge 1 – Silver

ACKNOWLEDGEMENTS

Sincere gratitude to you, Ayeisha, for being so open, honest and overly generous with your time in the research of this book.

To say that I thoroughly enjoyed our countless chats is an understatement in itself, I can certainly see why you are such an inspiration to so many.

Kudos to Ivan O'Brien for his support of the idea for this book, and for allowing me to turn a spotlight on the sport of hockey, and on one of its best and brightest stars.

Special thanks to the O'Brien Press team, the media for the mentions, and the booksellers for giving this title their attention.

Thank you to the powers-that-be at Hockey Ireland, Ulster Hockey, Leinster Hockey, Connacht Hockey and of course to my Munster Hockey family, who took a Dubliner under their wing and schooled him on the ins and outs of this great, and sometimes undervalued, sport.

Finally, to my own family, who stopped hitting the hockey ball against the office wall long enough for me to get some words down on paper. You will always be my favourite team.

ALSO AVAILABLE

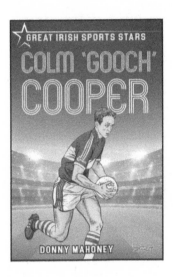

The Gaelic footballer who's won nearly every prize in the game:
Including 5 All-Irelands & 8 All-Stars

How a boy who everyone said wasn't big enough or strong
enough to wear the green and gold jersey of Kerry became one of
the greatest Gaelic footballers of all time.

ALSO AVAILABLE

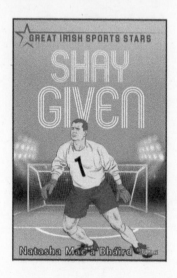

The inspiration behind many of Ireland's greatest days, Shay
Given earned 134 caps for his country and played in goal for
Ireland for 20 years! Follow Shay Given through the highs and
lows of a football career, playing in the Premier League, European
Championships and the World Cup. The story of one of Ireland's
greatest ever footballers.

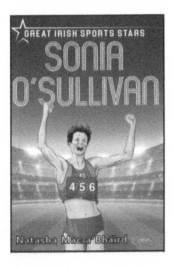

ALSO AVAILABLE

Through her talent, dedication and her ability to get back up and
dust herself down when things went wrong. Sonia went from an
ordinary girl who loved to run to an extraordinary world class
athlete.

The story of one of Ireland's greatest ever athletes -- and a dream
made real.

ALSO AVAILABLE

Cora Staunton is an elite sportswoman: a trailblazer in the
Australian Football League, and a hero in her native Mayo for
her gaelic football skills. But it's been a long and eventful road for
Cora. Discover how a girl playing with under-12 boys became a
living legend.

ALSO AVAILABLE

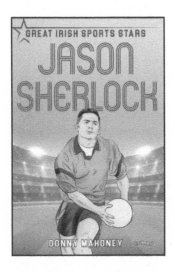

The inspiring story of how a boy from Dublin's northside found strength in his difference to become a Gaelic football great. Choosing GAA over basketball, soccer and hurling, 'Jayo' inspired a generation of fans and players. He went on to be a key member of Jim Gavin's five-in-a-row backroom team.